ALSO

DARCY COATES

DARCY COATES

Poisoned Pen
PRESS

Copyright © 2016, 2022 by Darcy Coates
Cover and internal design © 2022 by Sourcebooks
Cover design by Dane at EbookLaunch
Cover art by The Book Designers
Internal design by Holli Roach/Sourcebooks

Sourcebooks and the colophon are registered trademarks of Sourcebooks.

Published by Poisoned Pen Press, an imprint of Sourcebooks
P.O. Box 4410, Naperville, Illinois 60567–4410
(630) 961-3900
sourcebooks.com

Originally self-published in 2017 by Black Owl Books.

Cataloging-in-Publication Data is on file with the Library of Congress.

Printed and bound in the United States of America.
VP 10 9 8 7 6 5 4 3 2 1

THE DOG'S GRAVE DIGGER

RICK SWERVED A FRACTION OF A SECOND TOO LATE. HIS CAR'S tires screamed, leaving black tracks on the asphalt. Then there was a muffled thump. Rick felt a jolt move through his body, and the car rocked to a halt.

For a moment, Rick didn't dare do anything except breathe. Then he swore, loudly, and threw open the door. His car's high beams sliced through the night darkness, leaving trails of pale gold on the road. The markings from his tires spread out in a lazy loop, starting where he'd first seen the dog and ending three feet too late.

Rick knelt beside his car and looked over the result of his accident. The lumpy, bloody clump of fur was definitely dead and was barely recognizable as a dog. *The impact must have killed it instantly. Thank goodness for small blessings.* Rick grimaced and felt around its neck, but it didn't have a collar.

A stray, then? It does look thin.

Something about its nose, though, made him think it was a purebred. It might have been a stray when he'd hit it—he suspected it was because there weren't any houses for a twenty-minute drive in each direction—but it had probably been someone's pet at one time.

Rick swore again and pulled off his jacket. He'd lost a dog of his own when he was a child. The driver hadn't even stopped. The inhumanity had cut him deeply, and even twenty years later, he couldn't imagine leaving the animal on the side of the road. If it had belonged to a child, that child would want his pet treated respectfully.

The body mostly hung together, though one of the legs was only attached by a strip of flesh and a few muscles. Rick shrugged out of his jacket—*good thing I'm wearing the cheap one tonight*—and wrapped it around the dog, then carefully lifted the bundle into the passenger seat.

He returned to the driver's seat and hesitated as he tried to decide what to do with the animal. He could take it to a vet and hope they disposed of it kindly. Or he could take it home and bury it in his backyard. *Or...*

Rick put the car into gear, a smile growing across his face as he remembered what he had stored in the trunk. He'd bought a full set of gardening equipment the week before and hadn't gotten around to moving it out of his car. In among the shears, spades, and gloves was a shovel. And surrounding him was a forest.

Yes, a burial in the woods, where its body will nurture the trees. It's the best thing to do.

Rick drove until he found a gap in the trees wide enough for him to maneuver the car into. He drove past it then reversed, so that the back of the car would be facing the woods. He was able to get the car about twenty paces into the forest before it became too thick for him to continue. It wasn't quite far enough to disguise his car if a wayward driver happened to look in his direction, but at least it was more private than leaving his vehicle on the road. He hoped no one would see him. Goodness knew what a passer-by might think if they saw a lone man digging a hole in the woods at a quarter past midnight.

Rick turned off the car, smothering the headlights. The moon was full and bright, and the trees were sparse enough to let plenty of natural illumination through. The fallen pine needles crunched under his feet as he rounded his car and opened the trunk. Inside were the tools lying on a tarpaulin. He took the shovel, walked ten paces to a clear patch of ground, and started digging.

The dirt was tightly packed, but not as bad as he'd been expecting. Even so, it was exhausting work, and he started sweating before the hole was deeper than his arm.

It's got to be deep enough, he thought, *so the wild animals can't smell it and dig it out.*

The air was frosty, and his breath plumed in front of his face every time he exhaled. He knew his fingers would have become numb if the exercise hadn't been pumping blood through them so quickly.

A car came down the road, and Rick froze. The vehicle was traveling quickly, though, and passed Rick's hiding place without slowing down.

The rural road was rarely traveled, even during the day. Rick hadn't passed any cars during the last ten minutes of his drive, so he didn't expect to be disturbed again.

He dug until the sweat stained the underarms and back of his T-shirt and stuck his dark hair to his forehead. He'd made a good hole, a little larger than the dog would need and deep enough that the bones wouldn't come up for a long time. *Everyone deserves peace.*

Panting, his limbs trembling from the exertion, Rick climbed out of the hole and turned back to the car. Instead of going to the jacket-wrapped bundle in the passenger seat, he went to the trunk and pushed the tools off the tarpaulin. Then he grabbed the corner of the blue material and pulled it out of the trunk, straining against the weight. *Dead weight.* He chuckled to himself as he hauled his baggage toward the hole.

She'd go in with the tarpaulin, of course. A little extra insurance to protect her from being dug up. The tarpaulin couldn't be traced back to him; he'd bought it two states away at the same time as the tools—a complete set, to ensure there was no suspicion—and paid with cash. As far as anyone knew, the last time he'd seen his wife was that morning, when she'd kissed him on the cheek and left for work. Her car would be found abandoned at the train station the following day.

Rick gave the bundle a final shove and watched it tumble into the hole. Then he returned to the passenger seat of the car and drew the dog out with significantly more care. The dog had never cheated on him. The dog had never lied to him. In all likelihood, the dog had never even had a malicious thought. He knelt on the edge of the grave and laid the animal's body on top of his wife's, then he set to pouring the mound of dirt over the pair of them.

We all need rest.

KNOCKER

KARLA USED A PADDLE TO PUSH OFF FROM THE SHORE. THE
canoe rocked as it swept past the rushes clustered around the lake's
border and entered the clear water. The icy-cold wind snapped at
her exposed skin, but the jacket she'd brought protected her from
the worst of the chill.

Night creatures wailed mournfully from the forests bordering the lake, but their calls became increasingly remote as Karla
steered her canoe toward the lake's center. The moon wasn't quite
full, but it was close, and the light created odd ripples across the
water where her paddle disturbed its surface.

Once she was far enough into the lake that the cabin's lights
were a faint glow, Karla pulled her paddle back into the boat.
The canoe continued to roll in the tiny waves she'd created, but
it gradually stilled. The air was calm, and in the distance, the
water was still enough to act as a mirror for the sky. Its surface

was dotted with thousands of stars. It had been years since Karla had visited the remote lake, and she was always astounded at how clear the night was without light pollution or smog clouding it.

She folded her hands in her lap, closed her, eyes, and began to hum. The tune brought back a rush of memories from her childhood. She and her friends had sung it every time they'd gone on the lake, and she found it easy to remember their faces: Clarice, Peta, and Cass, beaming, laughing, and splashing water at each other. *It's been so long since I last saw them, last spoke to them. Time slips by faster with each passing year.*

From what she'd heard, no one went on the lake anymore. She'd even passed some aged warning signs on the way to the cabin. The water wasn't safe to swim in, the signs insisted.

Not that a sign was enough to deter Karla. Her family had virtually lived on the lake when she was a child; some government official who had probably never camped under the open night sky had no right to tell her where she could and couldn't tread.

She closed her eyes as she continued the mournful tune. The boat had been drifting while she sat, and the forest's noises were now inaudible under the gentle lapping and her hums.

Something scratched on the boat's underside. It was so faint that Karla almost didn't hear it. She snapped her eyes open and looked across the lake. Everything was still.

Probably a fish.

She resumed the tune and leaned back. The air still felt cold, but she was slowly adjusting to it. She knew her fingers would be numb by the end of an hour, but she didn't intend to stay on the lake for that long.

The brushing noise repeated. Karla didn't move, but her eyes snapped toward the boat's hull, to the section of wood that separated her from the creature below. The noise had been too loud and too drawn-out to be a fish—unless it was a very large, very slow fish.

Karla wet her lips. She glanced behind herself toward the shore, where the cabin lights glittered in the dark. She was the only one on the lake that week. With the water off-limits, holidaying families had moved on to more inviting camps.

The sound came once again, only this time it was accompanied by a scraping. It sounded like long, dull claws drawing across the boat's hull.

Karla's breathing was shallow. Sweat broke out across her already-cold skin. She wanted to pull her legs off the wooden base, but instead, she reached for the paddle. She raised it too quickly; one end bumped the boat's side.

She froze, her heart throbbing against her ribs, knuckles white on the paddle's wooden handle. There was perfect silence for a second—a quiet so deep and so vast that Karla's ears rang with it—then a solid *thud* shook the canoe. Her knock had been answered.

There was no one to hear her scream, even if she'd had enough moisture in her mouth to make a noise. Karla dunked the paddle over the canoe's side and dragged it through the water. She managed two strokes toward land before the paddle was seized.

Karla gasped and tried to tug it free. She was able to pull it partway out of the water before the pressure increased, dragging it from her hands and sweeping it deep into the lake, where it would likely never be recovered.

Without the paddle, she was stranded in the lake's center. Karla twisted in her seat, her eyes straining to see movement through the dark. *There!* Water to her left rippled as something moved through it. The shape disappeared as it drew closer, and then a slow, horrific scraping sound ran along the underside of the boat, starting at one side, drawing below Karla with agonizing slowness, and ending on her other side. Ripples disturbed the mirrorlike water.

She wanted to squeeze her eyes closed and clamp her hands over her ears to block out the sound, but she knew doing that would be suicide. She hunkered low in the canoe, hands resting on the clutter of shapes in its base, as shivers ran through her.

The world was quiet and still. Karla's breath plumed with every exhale, and her heart continued to thunder, but everything else was perfectly calm. She could almost think she'd imagined the whole thing.

Then the unseen visitor hit the boat hard enough that Karla would have been thrown over if she'd been standing. She exhaled a grunt as she hit the wooden side. The boat twirled like a leaf in the water. Another bump came from the other side, sending her careening in the opposite direction. Karla tightened her hands on the wood below her to keep her seat. The visitor was trying to throw her out of the canoe, and she clung on with every ounce of strength she possessed. The idea of being cast into the ink-black lake, her legs kicking feverishly as she fought to reach land, a waiting morsel for the unseen visitor, made her heart freeze.

The boat spiraled wildly, twirling in place, then was snapped to a halt. Karla blinked back tears as she searched the rolling water for the eyes she knew were about to appear.

The creature rose out of the lake. It was perfectly silent except for the water dripping off its misshapen form. The eyes—hundreds of them, all human, scattered erratically over its pulsing, off-gray hide—swiveled to look at her.

She thought she recognized a pair. Child-sized, the exact shade of blue that Clarice had possessed, bulging in the same way Clarice's had in those last moments.

They had thought they were being brave by leaving camp in the middle of the night. Their parents had been asleep, and they were eager to reach the opposite shore and explore the woods before going home. Peta's paddle had been pulled out of her hands as they neared the lake's center. Confused, she'd leaned over the boat's edge to peer into the water. She'd been pulled in.

Then came the scraping and the rocking. Cass had tried to stand and toppled over the edge. Clarice and Karla had clung to each other in the boat's base as the bulging-eyed creature rose out of the water, reached forward, plucked Karla's friend out of her arms—

At first, she hadn't known why she had been spared that night. It was only during the following years that a sense of purpose had come over her.

Karla's fingers tightened around the wood in her hands. She lifted the harpoon, a decade of practice and the throbbing adrenaline making the barbed spear seem to weigh nothing, and turned to face the visitor. Hundreds of eyes from countless lost souls stared at her, lidless and unblinking, and Karla stepped forward to claim her revenge.

SIXTH FLOOR

I SHOULD'VE COME EARLIER IN THE DAY.

Jack took his hands out of his leather jacket pockets and rubbed them together. The towering abandoned apartment building was shrouded in shadows at that late hour, and it was impossible to see through the windows on the sixth floor.

He turned to look at the building across the street. Hutchison and Proud, Attorneys at Law. The noble name belied a fundamentally seedy business that barely scraped by in the slummy downtown suburb. But his girlfriend, Cammi, worked there as a secretary.

Jack turned back to the abandoned apartments. The front door was boarded over. He knew there would be other ways to get in—broken windows and ledges and doors without locks—but the thin plywood was rotting from age and had fractured with a solid kick. It felt good to break something. Cammi had been upset for weeks about what she saw through the sixth-floor windows, and her constant crying had built a tension in Jack that could only be solved through violence.

Inside, the foyer was full of dust and long-abandoned cobwebs. A scrabbling sound came through one of the gaping black doorways. A rat, probably. Jack rubbed the back of his hand across his nose and glowered at the dark area.

The building had been vacant for more than ten years. It was in such bad disrepair that Cammi claimed it would be cheaper to knock it down and build a new building than to renovate it. But the downtown suburb already had too much housing for its dwindling population. Whoever owned the apartments must have given them up as a lost cause.

Broken glass, tiles, and dusty plaster coated the staircase and scraped under Jack's shoes as he climbed. His footsteps rang through the space, echoing eerily back at him from a dozen directions and blending in with his labored breathing. He'd been unemployed too long, he decided. The flab from too many beers and days spent in front of the television was setting in, and his heart had to work harder to lift him up the stairwell.

He repeated Cammi's words under his breath as he counted the floors. "In the window opposite my office." That would mean the sixth floor, near the building's corner. "He just stands there and stares at me all day."

He won't after this. Jack squeezed his fingers into fists. He would teach the creep a lesson. It didn't matter if it was a drugged-out hobo, a runaway teen, or just a run-of-the-mill pervert. If they didn't swear to stay away from the window, he would tip them over the sill and let them smack into the concrete sidewalk. The police wouldn't care. Deaths were common in the area, and unless they were blatant murders or easy to solve, they were mostly swept under the rug.

The stairwell opened onto the sixth floor, and Jack paused to catch his breath. The empty hallway stretched ahead of him, sad and decaying. Half the rooms were missing doors, and wan dying sunlight came through them. The whole area smelled of urine, rot, and sickening organic decay. He sniffed, rubbed at his nose again, then set out down the hallway, counting the rooms as he passed them.

It'll be one of the windows furthest along. Second or third from the corner room, probably. That would look directly out at Cammi's window.

He peered into each room. A couple still held furniture, though they were so badly damaged that they would be worthless. Rat droppings were thick on the ground. One room showed signs of being lived in within the last few years, but dust clung to the mattress, suggesting the owner had moved on some time ago.

At last, at the hallway's second-to-last room, Jack found he was no longer alone. A figure, tall and thin, was silhouetted against the light. Standing at the window, he stared out at the street below.

Jack's heart raced, but he drew in a breath to spread his chest. He placed a hand on each side of the doorway, blocking the stranger's escape, and bellowed, "Oy!"

The figure didn't reply and didn't move. Something about it struck Jack as unnatural. No human could keep that still; it wasn't even breathing. He held his pose in the doorway for a moment, watching it, then cautiously stepped into the room.

As soon as the light was no longer behind the figure, it became clear. The shock and relief caused a laughing fit, and Jack doubled over as he hacked in breaths and drew a shaking hand through his hair. It was just a mannequin.

Jack moved up to it and poked the cold porcelain skin as his chuckles gradually subsided. "Jeez, buddy, you've been terrorizing my girl for weeks."

He pulled out his cell phone, took a photo of the figure, and sent it to Cammi with the caption, "Found the creep opposite your window. He's a real dummy!"

It was a good pun, Jack thought as he turned toward the window and stared at Cammi's workplace. He could barely see the little cactus she kept at her window. She'd been right; the figure was almost perfectly opposite. He wondered idly if someone had left the mannequin as a prank or if it had just been abandoned like the other furniture.

His phone buzzed with a reply message. "What the hell? Did you actually go there?" quickly followed by "You promised you wouldn't. It's not safe." The phone buzzed a third time. "And that's not the window guy. He doesn't just stand still. Sometimes he paces."

Jack frowned at the final message then drew a sharp breath as a hand landed on his shoulder.

THE SIGHTLESS

MEAGHAN SAT IN THE PLUSH ARMCHAIR BESIDE THE WINDOW and watched the streets. A number of figures had passed within the last half hour. They'd moved out of and faded back into the mist like phantoms, never lingering. Even though the street was empty, she didn't dare relax.

Seeing her town so quiet was surreal. There were no more dogs left to bark. No car horns blared. None of her neighbors argued or started their lawnmowers, even though it was Sunday morning. At least, she thought it was Sunday morning. She was starting to lose track.

Taj approached from behind. He'd shed his shoes in favor of layered socks, and she wasn't aware of him until he leaned over her shoulder and passed her a note.

Is it safe to open a can?

Meaghan slipped a pen out of her pocket and carefully wrote back, *I think so. Haven't seen any for a few minutes.*

Taj nodded and returned to the kitchen, his padded feet making no more noise than Meaghan's heartbeat. That was important. In this new world, the world of the Sightless, noise equaled death.

No one was completely sure where they'd come from. The earliest news reports—the ones that had made it through before the media blackout—said they'd poured out of mines that had gone too deep. A few people called them aliens, though that was an unpopular phrase, as they'd come from inside earth. Others called them demons, but they had very little in common with the demons Meaghan had been raised to believe in. Meaghan and her two companions, Taj and Lisa, called them Sightless.

They couldn't see, and they couldn't smell, though they somehow seemed quite comfortable navigating the suburban neighborhood. The only way they could find their prey—humans—was through sound.

Meaghan didn't know how many people were still alive in her street. Possibly none. Before the media blackout—before the creatures had rushed through her town like a deadly wave—there had been stories of entire cities being overrun. She hadn't seen any of her neighbors for more than a day.

She was lucky, she knew. Her parents had been preppers. That hadn't saved them from the Sightless... but at least it had ensured Meaghan's pantry was filled with cans of long-life food and five-liter jugs of water. It was enough to keep herself, Taj, and Lisa alive for a few weeks, at least.

There damn well better be a rescue before those weeks are up.

She had no idea how the rest of the world was faring. For all she knew, the military was deploying weapons against the Sightless at that very moment. On the other hand, humanity might have been all but destroyed and reduced to little pockets of survivors like in Meaghan's house. Not speaking. Walking with silent care. Terrified that at any moment a sneeze or a cough could force their hand.

Meaghan glanced behind herself to where Taj had taken a large can of beans out of the cupboard. Lisa stood leaning on the counter, her long tan hair hiding half of her face. While Taj was a longtime friend, Meaghan didn't know much about Lisa—only that she'd stumbled into their house on the night the Sightless had invaded and was grateful they'd allowed her to stay with them.

Taj eased the can's ring up then began tugging the lid free of its seal with slow, gentle motions. Opening cans was always a risk. Sometimes they were perfectly silent, but other times, the metal whined. They tried to reduce their risk by waiting until there weren't any Sightless in the streets, but mist had rolled through that morning and reduced Meaghan's visibility to less than a dozen feet.

Taj had the lid halfway off when it let out a high-pitched squeal. He froze, and his eyes bugged. Meaghan rose to her feet and stared at the window, praying that there hadn't been any Sightless close enough to hear.

One of the creatures slunk through the mist, its eyeless, nose-less face turned toward her window. A second followed not far behind. Meaghan couldn't even breathe the swearword that hung on her tongue.

The window's glass had been broken out on the night of the invasion. Meaghan's parents had tried to fight back. Their bodies were gone, but the blood would never come out of the walls.

Meaghan took an involuntary step backward, holding her breath and praying her heartbeat wouldn't be audible. The first Sightless stepped easily over the window's sill. Its long, leathery gray legs were as silent as Meaghan wished her human limbs could be. It passed her so closely that she could smell the decaying flesh that tainted its breath. Its mouth, a long gash covering the otherwise-empty, tapered face opened a fraction, exposing the off-white teeth inside.

It moved through the house with deceptive slowness. Meaghan had seen how quickly they could run when they pinpointed a noise. *Faster than a cheetah.*

The second Sightless climbed over the sill. Meaghan realized its trajectory meant it would bump into her, and she took a careful step to her left. For a moment, she was afraid that, even with her feet double-layered in thick socks, she'd been too fast and made a noise. The Sightless hesitated for a second, its head tilted in her direction, then continued toward the kitchen.

Taj was sweating and shaking. He'd left the can on the counter and held his hands at his sides in the pose they'd discovered worked best to stop shifting clothing noises. He stared straight ahead, his lips clenched shut, as the Sightless wove toward him. He was holding his breath, and drops of sweat beaded over his face.

He's frightened. They'll hear his heart.

Meaghan squeezed her eyes closed, unwilling to watch, as the Sightless homed in on her friend. Then shattering glass in a building across the street broke the silence. The Sightless froze for a fraction of a second, then both turned and shot through the room as gray blurs. They passed so near Meaghan that she felt the wind ruffle her hair. The creatures leaped through the window and crossed the street in two paces as they raced toward the unfortunate soul who had been careless enough to make a noise.

Meaghan finally inhaled, drawing breath into her starving lungs, and turned toward the kitchen. Taj had both hands pressed over his face and was shivering.

As their unknown neighbor's screams rose into a terrified, agonized wail, Lisa picked up the half-opened can and offered it and a spoon to Meaghan. She tried to return the grim smile and scooped a spoonful of beans. She was practical enough to know there would be no safer time to eat than when any noises were masked by the screams.

FLOTSAM

A BODY LAY AMONG THE ROCK POOLS.

Leisi froze, one hand clutching her beach bag, the other halfway through wiping strands of hair out of her eyes. She stared at the shape.

The bluff offered a good view of the rock-dotted beach and dark rolling ocean. When she'd left her hotel that morning, it had been a clear spring day. Blue skies, fluffy clouds, and a warm breeze had encouraged her to keep her plans for a visit to the beach, even though the café server had warned bad weather was coming. Dark clouds had begun to gather not long after Leisi left the town.

She hadn't realized just how remote the beach was. She lived in Sydney, where a hot day meant every sandy cove was packed with sunbathers and families. But this was New Zealand and a good way out from the touristy areas. The beach looked as though it almost never saw human intervention. She'd even passed a group of seals happily sunning themselves on the rocks a few kilometers back.

Maybe that's what the shape is: a seal. Sailors used to mistake them for mermaids, didn't they? Leisi squinted at the shape. *Definitely human.* There were no flippers or oily skin, but two arms dragged through the rock pools as the waves nudged at the figure.

Leisi turned to the path that led to the town, but hesitated. The walk back would take more than an hour. Thick clouds were already turning the sky's cornflower blue into gray as the storm swelled.

The body rocked in a mesmerizing cycle as the water lapped around it. She didn't think it had caught on any rocks; if the tide pulled it out, it would be lost again, possibly forever. *I can't let that happen.*

The incline leading to the rocky shore was steep, and Leisi tightened her grip on her bag before sitting on the edge of the grassy overhang and swinging her feet over the edge. She slid down the slope, regained her feet, and jogged toward the shape swaying in the water.

It was wearing dark-blue clothes. Some sort of uniform, Leisi thought, though the fabric was tattered from being snagged in the rocky surf. He might have fallen from one of the freighters that circled the islands or possibly even a cruise ship.

As Leisi moved closer, the intense smell hit her, making her stomach muscles clench and her throat restrict. She tried to breathe through her mouth, but the odor became stuck on her tongue. Under the torn clothes, his skin was bubbling—*swelling*—as bacteria worked on converting the flesh into gas. He lay facedown in the water, so she couldn't see his expression, but his scalp had lost a lot of its hair.

Get him onto the beach. Get him secured. Then go for help.

Leisi knelt beside the body. The smell made her retch, and she pressed her right sleeve over her nose as she reached her spare hand toward the corpse. Thunder cracked overhead. It was close; so close that she knew she would certainly get drenched on the walk back to the town.

Squeezing her eyes until they were nearly closed, Leisi touched the corpse's shoulder. The cloth, cold and wet, felt slimy under her fingers. She wanted to move back and to look away, but she didn't allow herself. Instead, she tightened her grip on the jacket and pulled.

The body was heavier than she'd expected. Its clothes caught in the rocks, and its head lolled, spilling water out of its open mouth and the holes pocking its skin. With the water came more of the smell.

She'd never thought a decaying human could be so overwhelming. Leisi gagged as she pulled the figure out of the water and dragged it farther up the beach. She didn't let herself stop until she'd reached the curve where the beach rose into the bluff, then she let go and stepped back with a gasp of relief.

The body was missing a leg. Leisi's heart dropped. She glanced at the water's edge, where the limb floated, half-submerged in the sea-foamed rock pool.

I can't just leave it there.

Leisi approached the leg. The pants had stayed with the body, leaving the limb exposed. It looked ghastly: gray, bubbling, and eaten away in many sections where sea creatures had feasted. Touching the flesh was abhorrent. It was slimy and spongy, with just enough of the familiar fleshy texture to retrigger Leisi's gag reflex. She carried it up the beach as quickly as she could and left it beside the body.

Another crack of thunder deafened her as the sky lit up. Leisi turned to the ocean, where the waves were rolling closer, growing in size, and breaking on the bank of rocks near the shore. A huge, heavy raindrop hit her face.

The waves would sweep into the cove as the storm grew. If the police decided to wait until after the storm, the body might be washed away by the time they reached the beach. Leisi stared at the waterlogged corpse. *It had been a person, who might have a family. And who deserves a proper funeral. I can't let him be lost again.*

She searched along the shore for rocks. Most of them were too large to lift, but she found half a dozen small stones, which she wedged around the corpse to weigh it down. *Will that be enough? What if it's not? I should find something to bring back for the police to identify the body, at least.*

Leisi knelt beside the figure and held her breath while she searched the uniform's pockets. If he'd been carrying a wallet, it had been lost to the ocean. As she felt around the jacket, something else came loose, and Leisi stared at it for a moment before deciding. *That will have to do.*

She tugged the item free then stepped away from the body, stifling her gag reflex. Leisi carefully placed her prize into the beach bag. *This way, even if the body's gone by the time they find the beach, they'll have something. Something to identify. Something to bury.*

The rain had started to fall in earnest. With a final glance at the body, Leisi scrambled up the slope. She reached the path at the top, wiped her wet hair out of her face, and began the long walk back to town, the corpse's head tucked snugly in her beach bag.

GREAT-AUNT ENID

JACOB SAT IN HIS CAR, STARING AT THE HOUSE'S FRONT. SINGLE-story and narrow, it looked as though it could only hold three or four rooms. The plants in the front garden were almost dead, save for a bunch of straggling weeds that had survived under the dripping tap. The house's windows were all blinded with dark shutters, and the walls were stained from age.

And yet, it still held hints of nostalgia. Jacob could picture flowers filling the front garden and imagine the large, now-lifeless elm tree full of bright-green leaves in early spring. He remembered his great-aunt, her blue eyes shining behind her glasses, as she held his hand and walked with him to the park.

These twenty years haven't been kind to the house. What will they have done to Aunt Enid?

Jacob sucked in a deep breath and stepped out of his car. The leaves crunched under his boots as he crossed the road and pushed open the ancient metal gate. It whined on its hinges and stuck at the halfway point. Jacob skirted it and followed the blackened pathway to where the house's front door, tall and faded, sat in the off-white plaster walls.

He rapped on the door and listened for the sounds of footsteps. Instead, a voice, cracked and raspy, called, "Come in."

Jacob paused before opening the door. He knew almost nothing about his great-aunt, save for a handful of bright childhood memories. Walking with her to the shops, coloring in books she'd bought for him, and being given a handful of lollies when his parents collected him to go home. He knew he'd spent a lot of time at her house as a toddler, but one day, the visits had just...*stopped.*

Jacob had almost forgotten about her until, cleaning out his mother's attic the weekend before, he'd come across a photo of his deceased grandmother and great-aunt sitting together.

He'd asked his parents about her, but they seemed reluctant to tell him what had happened. From what he could work out based on their evasive answers and uncomfortable pauses, some sort of falling out had occurred between Aunt Enid and the rest of his family.

"Haven't heard from her in decades," his father had said, and his mother had added, in an unusually sour tone, "She's probably still holed up in that house."

It hadn't been hard to track down her details; she'd lived in the building for her entire adult life. What had been strange, though, was how isolated she seemed. None of Jacob's cousins or uncles would talk about her, and if they did, they never said much except that she lived alone and didn't have friends.

That had struck Jacob as wrong in many ways. No matter what the disagreement had been about, an elderly lady living alone should have *some* sort of company. *Even if it's just a visit from a long-forgotten grandnephew.*

Jacob opened the door. It caught on the mat lining the hallway, and he had to shove it to get it to move. Inside, the house had a strange musty smell, with undertones of mildew. A grandfather clock somewhere farther in the building ticked. Jacob hesitated on the mat, then the voice repeated, "Come in."

He remembered Aunt Enid's voice as being melodic and smooth and her having a good, strong laugh. What called to him was dry and raspy.

I was right—she's not well. I can't believe my family would leave her here like this. She should have someone check in on her a few times a week, at least.

Jacob closed the door behind himself and followed the hallway. The house hadn't looked large from the outside, but the hall went on much farther than he'd expected before it opened into a sitting room.

His Aunt Enid sat in the chair under the window. At first glance, she looked like a shadow; her black dress pooled around her feet, and her once-black hair, which had aged to steel gray, hung around her face in a long, greasy sheet. She sat immobile, her hands lying limply in her lap, her face turned toward the discolored glass.

Jacob cleared his throat. "Aunt Enid?" he asked, taking a step into the room. "Hi, it's me—"

"Jacob," she said, her aged, wrinkled mouth framing the word carefully. "I didn't expect to see you again."

Though her hands stayed limp in her lap, she turned her torso and head toward him, moving slowly, as though her joints were rusty.

Jacob smiled awkwardly. "Uh, yeah. It's—it's good to see you again."

Her eyes were milky white. *Blind. Why didn't anyone tell me? How can she possibly be living alone like this?*

Enid raised one of her hands and indicated to the seat opposite. The hand was curled like a bird's claw, so aged and stiff with arthritis that it was clearly difficult to move.

Jacob sat in the chair, trying to ignore how dusty and stained it was. He leaned forward, cleared his throat, and tried to inject some life into his voice. "I have so many happy memories of visiting you as a child. I'm sorry we lost touch."

"Hmm." Enid's head had followed his movements, even though Jacob knew she couldn't see him. "Your family didn't agree with...some of my choices."

Curiosity gnawed at Jacob. No one had given a reason for the rift, but he knew it had to be dramatic. His family was generally tight-knit. To outright ignore his aging great-aunt...he couldn't believe it. "Choices?" he prompted.

She smiled, exposing a row of surprisingly straight white teeth. *Dentures, surely.*

"Choices you wouldn't even consider," she said, and turned back to stare out of the window. Jacob wondered if that was how she passed her days: staring blindly into the yard for hours on end until hunger or thirst drove her into movement. "Choices you wouldn't even imagine could exist." The unnatural smile again stretched her wrinkled lips until they cracked.

What could she possibly mean? What sort of choices did she have to make? Jacob was starting to feel uncomfortable, so he changed the subject to the main purpose of his visit. The sentiment was difficult to express, so he chose his words carefully. "Enid, do you have anyone to visit you? Maybe a neighbor who can pop in every few days?"

Enid acted as though she hadn't heard him. Her face had taken on a strange, intense expression as she stared at the window, and her voice dropped to a whisper. "It was a different time back then. When you were offered something impossible, you didn't always question it."

Jacob stared at his clasped hands. "If…if it's okay with you… I was thinking I could drop by every now and then. I work at a store only about ten minutes away, so if you'd like some company, I could come by after my shifts—"

"Jacob," she said, as though reminding herself of his name. "Do as your family did. It's no good for you to spend time with those who have bartered with their souls."

"It's no trouble," Jacob said hurriedly as his aunt tried to rise from her chair. "Really, it would be nice to see more of you… and, I mean, if anything were to happen…"

"Ha." It was a cold, hollow laugh. Enid had gotten to her feet and moved around her chair. She was walking strangely, as though her joints had frozen while she sat. Movement on the floor caught Jacob's eyes, and he saw fleshy, white objects had fallen from the folds of his great-aunt's dress. They squirmed on the floor. *Surely those aren't...maggots?*

Aunt Enid turned her head to stare at Jacob, and he realized, with a jolt, that she *could* see him despite the bleached-white eyes. "No," she said, scraping toward him laboriously. "You'll do better to spend your time with the living."

RED MORNING

THE FEED BUCKETS WERE HEAVY IN ALLEN'S HANDS AS HE CROSSED the yard toward the chicken coop. The sun was barely touching the ground, and the area was dull in the early-morning half-light. He'd already fed and milked the cows and could hear the chickens fussing about their cage's door as he neared them.

Allen paused and turned toward the woods' edge forty paces away. Crow cawing drifted across the space, and a flutter of wings just behind the tree line caught his attention. Something had died there during the night, and the birds were feasting.

A fox? Allen left the feed buckets beside the coop and crossed to the woods' edge. Foxes had killed six of his chickens before he'd poisoned them out of the area. If they'd returned, he would need to set out new baits. The dead animal had to be large, based on the number of flapping, screeching birds, and as he drew closer, Allen's mind shifted from fox to bear.

The figure was made of patchy browns and pinks, but the birds' massacre had been so thorough that it wasn't until he was nearly on top of it that Allen recognized it as human. The world seemed to fall abruptly still, and for a moment, all Allen could do was stare, tight-lipped, at the stained fur jacket, torn jeans, matted hair, and fleshy limbs reaching out. Then one of the birds fluttered up to dig at the woman's face, and something inside Allen snapped. He grabbed a branch off the forest floor and waved it at the crows to scatter them. They hopped out of reach, their beady eyes alternately watching their meal and Allen's weapon as they cackled and cawed at him.

"Get away!" he yelled, swinging the branch again, but he knew they wouldn't stay back for long.

The woman's body seemed fresh. The birds had torn out her eye and tongue and had picked holes through her face, but they hadn't been at work long enough to disguise the blisters disfiguring her skin. The scabs looked angry and red, as though she'd fallen into boiling water. Allen realized he was staring and turned away, though he knew he would never forget the image.

He pulled his cell phone out of his jacket pocket but hesitated over the buttons. He was friendly with the local sheriff, but he didn't know if it would be appropriate to call Matt or if he was supposed to phone the emergency helpline directly. He suspected it was the latter, but that felt too impersonal. He dialed Matt instead. Their town was large enough to see accidental deaths and even the occasional murder; Matt would know what to do.

The phone rang and rang. That wasn't too unusual. It was

early in the morning, and the sheriff could be in the shower or even still sleeping. Allen waited for the answering machine and said, "It's Allen. Call me back. It's important." Than he reluctantly hung up and dialed the emergency helpline.

The crows cackled as they hopped nearer to the body. Allen swiped his branch at them again then frowned as an engaged tone beeped in his ear. He lowered his cell phone and looked at it. The emergency helpline was nonresponsive.

He blinked, scanned the area, and tried redialing. The result was the same. Allen swore under his breath and tucked the phone into his pocket. He'd need to go to town.

Allen didn't want to touch or move the unnamed woman, but he couldn't stomach leaving her for the crows, either, so he spent some time finding fallen branches and piling them over her form. He stacked them deep enough that a bird would have trouble getting through, then sent the ring of waiting crows a glower before turning toward his road.

His farm was on the outskirts of town but along a main highway. Allen made for the road, thinking it would save some time if he could hitchhike in, but the highway was empty at that early hour. He jogged along the asphalt, his heartbeat throbbing in his ears and his lungs starved for oxygen. He was still a kilometer from town when he came across the car.

It was an old blue model that had run off the road. Its nose was wedged into the ditch, leaving its back wheels hanging in the air. Allen slowed as he neared it then circled around until he was certain there was no fire that could make the fuel tank explode.

He peered through the windows, but the car was empty, save for a few empty chip packets and a discarded beanie. He made note of the paddock it had crashed in front of and calculated it would take a disoriented woman less than an hour to stumble across the field and through the woods before collapsing on Allen's property. It would explain how she'd gotten there, but not where the blisters had come from. He kept running.

Allen's mind was so occupied by his own problem that he was inside the town boundary before he realized how eerily silent it was. Shops that should have been open were empty and dark. The road was devoid of cars and people—even the few determined joggers who rose earlier than the farmers. Allen slowed to a walk and stared, open-mouthed, at the spectacle. It was almost as if he'd walked into some bizarre alternate world.

It took him several minutes to find another person. The barkeeper, a plump balding man who typically didn't go home until three in the morning, lay half in the gutter and half in the road. Allen approached but didn't touch him. The way the barkeep was sprawled would have made it look like he'd imbibed too much of his own drink…if not for the angry red blisters puckering his skin.

Nausea rose and coated Allen's tongue. He began backing away, moving back toward the town's border, then he froze as a distant siren pierced the quiet morning air. It sounded like it was coming from the next town.

Allen began running again, fear powering already-tired legs. He was just outside the town's border when he heard the jets overhead. He didn't slow his pace but lifted his eyes to see the crafts shoot over the town, spreading plumes of odd purple-tinted contrails in their wakes.

He pulled his scarf out of his jacket and wrapped it around his face, praying he could make it to the relative safety of his rural farm before the gas reached the ground.

FOOTSTEPS IN THE NIGHT

Denise woke from her dream, feeling as though she were clawing her way out of a deep, dark lake. Her brain felt sluggish, and she couldn't immediately understand what had disturbed her. Then sounds filtered through: footsteps shuffling on the cold tile floors of her kitchen.

Bernard mustn't be able to sleep. Again.

Denise stretched a hand behind herself and felt the familiar indent in the mattress. It was cold; her husband must have been up for a while. She wished he would come back to bed. After thirty years of marriage, she found it hard to fall asleep without company.

What time is it? Denise rolled forward to reach the lamp. Her fingers brushed a bottle, knocking it off the edge of the bedside table. The bottle's contents rattled as it hit the floor. *What's that?*

She already knew what it was, though. *Sleeping pills.* Her

mind, still filled with that deep-water sensation, couldn't remember why she had sleeping pills on her bedside table. She'd never suffered from insomnia. That was Bernard's quarter.

The footsteps moved from the kitchen to the lounge room in a path Denise was intimately familiar with. Every night, he stalked through their home, searching, perhaps for relief from his own mind. He always took the same route: from the hallway to the kitchen to the lounge room to the hallway to the spare room, then back again. Denise was so used to it that it almost never disturbed her anymore.

It's different tonight, though. He wasn't taking his usual care to move quietly, and his feet scraped over the carpet to produce harsh *shhh, shhh, shhh* sounds.

Denise's fingers found the lamp's button. The shadows scattered to the deepest corners of the room as illumination fell upon the familiar shapes. Her bureau, the beautiful wooden table that normally held her trinkets and a vase of fake flowers, was a mess. Someone had scattered the contents to the ground. Denise frowned. *Who? And why did I go to bed without tidying it?*

A faint blurred memory rose in her mind. She saw herself sweeping her forearm across the table, knocking off the makeup and silver brushes Bernard had given her, even the cherished necklace he'd bought her on their thirtieth anniversary.

Denise bent over the edge of the bed to pick up the bottle she'd knocked to the floor. It was unexpectedly light. She shook it and found it was only half-full. *I've been taking them for a few days, then. They must be the reason my head's so foggy. I can't remember…*

The shuffling footsteps moved through the lounge room. Denise imagined her husband, his sagging face cold and distant as he gazed out of the full-length window toward the swaying black trees that lined their driveway. He always looked grim when the insomnia had him in its grip. Once, not long after their marriage, she'd asked him why he looked that way. He'd stared at her for a long time without answering.

Shhh, shhh, shhh. Bare feet dragged over the carpet as Bernard's well-worn path took him past their bedroom. His silhouette appeared in the doorway, too far from her lamp for his features to find any relief, and finally, his pacing stopped.

Denise thought he might be ready to come back to bed, but he didn't enter the room. Though shadows obscured his face, she could make out the shock of thin, messy hair and the outline of his crumpled clothes.

"Bern?"

A strange odor accompanied him. She'd smelled it before, she knew, and recently, but she couldn't place where.

She still cradled the bottle of sleeping pills in her hand, and she squeezed it as images flashed across her sluggish mind: the flowers, anachronistically bright, lying across the dark polished wood. *That's what the smell is*, she realized. *He smells like those flowers.*

She saw herself sitting at the bureau and watching the tears run down her face, ruining the makeup, bleeding the black eyeliner and the rouge that had been intended to hide her paleness. She'd been surrounded by the gifts her husband had lavished on her, and it was intolerable, so she'd swept them off the table and watched them clatter to the ground.

Then she remembered standing on a grassy swell, staring into a black hole as the polished wood was lowered into it, and she realized why she'd needed the sleeping tablets. They were the only thing that had been able to bring her rest after the funeral.

After Bernard's funeral.

Denise turned toward the bedroom doorway, where the silhouetted man watched her.

SURF

MARINA LET THE FIRE BURN PATTERNS INTO HER VISION AS HER long, thin hair created curtains to hide her face. Her five friends, spaced around the seaside firepit, had all become chattier as the alcohol hit them—but drink only ever made Marina quieter and more self-conscious. She was happy to let the conversation flow over her as she tuned out the individual words.

Todd pushed away from the sand, where he'd been lying on his belly. His curly hair flopped around his face, reminding Marina of a shaggy dog, and she dipped her head a little farther to hide her smile.

"I'm gonna catch a couple more waves." His voice was faintly slurred, but if the beer had affected his coordination, it was impossible to tell it apart from his regular ungainliness. He stumbled toward the row of surfboards propped in the sand. "Who's coming?"

"Stay by the fire," said Elena, the self-appointed mother of the group. "Don't drink and drive a surfboard, boy."

He cackled a laugh and turned to Marina. "You wanna come? I'll teach you."

She mutely shook her head, so he shrugged and began jogging toward the ocean.

A second later, his best friend, James, also leaped out of the sand and grabbed his own surfboard. "Oy, wait up!"

Elena snorted and nudged Marina with an elbow. "Todd likes you, you know. That's the fourth time he's asked you to join him today."

"I don't like the ocean," Marina mumbled, hoping that would be enough to shut down the discussion.

Elena looked as if she wanted to talk more, but at that moment, Lari dropped her beer can into the fire, and the cries and laughter served as a distraction. Marina sat for a moment more, watching the flickering flames, then excused herself and rose.

She hadn't been drunk in a long time, and the alcohol was affecting her more than she'd expected. She went as far as the ocean's edge then began walking parallel to the surf, hoping the cool wind and exercise would sober her. To her right, Todd and James were paddling out toward the waves.

The shore was far enough from town that the tourists didn't often go there, and its pristine sand was littered with colorful shells. Marina bent to pick some up, a half-formed idea of turning them into a necklace hovering in the back of her mind. She'd only collected a handful when she saw something that didn't belong on the beach.

Her first thought was that it was a piece of coral. It was thin and only a few inches long, but the color didn't match anything that she would have expected to find in the sand. The waves lapped at it, and as it rolled, she saw its fingernail.

Marina opened her mouth to scream, but only a thin whine came out. She dropped the shells, glanced toward the fire, toward the ocean, then back down at the severed human finger drifting in the surf.

The alcohol was clogging her ability to reason, so she did the only thing she could think of. She reached forward, hesitated, then picked up the digit between two of her own fingers, holding it away from herself as she hurried back to the fire.

The three who had remained there were all laughing at something Lari had said, but Elena's smile vanished as Marina held the finger toward her. "Mar, what the hell!"

"I found it," Marina said helplessly, dropping it on the sand beside the fire. "In the water."

Lari gaped at her. "And you picked it up?"

"I didn't know what else to do!"

"Hang on." Elena had her palms pressed to her temple, her earlier intoxicated glow gone. "Calm down. We need to figure out what to do. Did you...uh...did you see any other body parts?"

Marina's horrified stare was all the answer Elena needed. She squeezed her eyes closed and scratched at her scalp. "Okay, so, maybe this happened in an accident. Or...or maybe it's from something worse."

"It's fresh." Peta pointed toward the severed edge. "Look, it's still red, and it hasn't started to decay yet. So it's probably from today. Maybe only a few hours old."

Elena's fingers were still scratching restlessly. "Okay. Okay. Who has a phone? We need to call the police."

"I do." Peta flipped over to dig through her bag.

"Great. We'll call the police, and…and…" Her attention turned toward the water, where Todd and James were surfing.

"You think they're in danger?" Lari asked.

"Well, fingers don't just drop off, do they?" Elena snapped. She stood, dusted sand off her shorts, then jogged toward the water's edge.

Marina followed. She'd heard there were sharks in the area, although they normally didn't come into the crescent beach. Once the idea had been suggested, it was impossible to forget.

"Oy!" Elena screamed across the waves. "Todd! James!"

The boys were a long way out, straddling their surfboards and facing the horizon. They didn't respond to the calls. Elena swore.

"Come back!" Marina, feeling the first real sting of panic, screamed so loudly, her voice cracked. "Todd!"

"They can't hear us." Elena was running her fingers through her hair again and shivering, despite the warm night. "Crap, they shouldn't have gone out so late—and they're drunk."

Lari shoved between them, dragging her own surfboard toward the waves. "I'll get them back."

"Crap, no, Lari—"

Elena's objections fell on deaf ears. Lari waded out as far as she could, then leaped onto the board and began paddling. Marina squeezed her hands together, watching her friend set a course toward the waves, as Elena paced beside her.

"It's probably fine," Marina said, but her voice sounded faint in her own ears. "Like you said, it was probably an accident or something."

"Peta's still on the phone." Elena folded her arms and shifted up onto her toes to watch Lari's board, then she turned abruptly. "I'll go see what they're saying."

Marina stayed by the ocean's edge, her eyes glued on the three figures bobbing in and out of view on the swell. Part of her was starting to wish she'd left the finger on the shore; it had caused much panic, and probably for nothing. She was sure there were a hundred ways someone could lose a finger—it didn't have to be sharks.

The two boys looked around as Lari neared them, and all three turned their surfboards back toward the beach. Marina began to breathe properly again. It would only take them a minute to reach shore, and then there would be nothing to worry about. She twisted toward the firepit to call out the good news, but it was vacant. Frowning, she moved cautiously toward it, trying to pick out either Elena or Peta in the dim light. Their bags, their bottles, and the packets of chips sat where they'd been left. Even the severed finger lay near the fire, its nail picking up a glimmer of light from the flames. But her friends were gone. In their place were five small drops of blood quivering in the sand.

Marina dashed into the ocean. She was waist-deep when Todd,

the nearest, reached her. "Pull me up!" She grabbed for his arm, begging to be let onto his board. "It's the beach that's dangerous, not the water. Pull me up!"

THOSE WHO LIVE IN THE WOODS

TESSA FLIPPED HER SLEEPING BAG OUT OF ITS HOLDER AND LAID IT beside Karin's. They had only a two-person tent, with barely enough room for their bags. Once Fel arrived, they would be like sardines in a can. Not that she minded. They'd been through worse on their annual long-weekend camping adventures, including one trip where their tent had been blown away and they'd had to sleep outdoors for two nights before making it back to civilization.

She poked her head out of the tent to see Karin sitting beside the fire, turning sausages on the skillet. "How're they doing?"

"Just about there." Karin was leaning so close to the flame that the flickering light seemed to make her face glow. She had the excited, almost manic smile she always wore whenever they started on their hikes. Even though the parking lot was only twenty meters behind them, she was glad to be among nature again. "Should be done by the time Fel gets here."

Tessa checked her watch. "She really should have been here by now. Unless her boss made her stay late."

"That guy's a jerk."

"Oh, he totally is."

Karin opened her mouth to say something more, but fell silent as she heard what sounded like squealing tires in the distance. "You don't think that's—"

The screeching stopped abruptly, but then, a moment later, she heard what sounded like breaking glass. Karin dropped her fork and rose. They both faced toward the parking lot, which was hidden by the forest and the darkness. The two friends glanced at each other, then Karin said, "I'll go check it out."

"Want me to come?"

"Nah." Karin grabbed the flashlight from where Tessa had left it beside the tent and switched it on. "I'll be back in a moment. Watch the sausages."

Tessa poked at the splitting sausage skins as she listened to her friend march through the forest. The light from the flashlight faded before the sound of her footsteps did. Then Karin started calling, "Fel? Fel! *Fe-e-el!*"

The night air was cooling rapidly, and Tessa snuggled closer to the fire as she waited. The logs, not quite dry enough for a calm blaze, spat and hissed as sap was cooked out of them. Karin had fallen quiet, which Tessa assumed meant she'd either found Fel or had given up.

The sounds of the woods were magnified in her friends' absence. Tessa gazed at the trees as the isolation started to bite at her. The trunks, dark and rough, stretched high above their camping ground, the leaves blocking out almost all of the stars. She felt as though she'd been transported to another dimension— one without other humans. She hated the idea.

Karin should be back by now, shouldn't she? Tessa checked her watch. Nearly fifteen minutes had passed since her friend had left. The parking lot was nowhere near far enough away for the trip to take that long. Tessa pulled the sausages—which were so overdone, they were drying out—off the fire and stood. "Karin?"

She half expected not to get a reply, but after a second, Karin returned her call. "Fel?"

She's still looking for her, then. Has something happened?

"Fel! Fel! Fe-e-el!"

"Karin?" Tessa yelled, projecting her voice as far as she could. "What's happening?"

"Fel! Fel!"

Tessa crossed her arms over her chest and waited. Karin's voice didn't resume, and she didn't reappear through the trees. Minutes ticked by. Tessa's anxiety rose with each passing second, until she couldn't stand it any longer. She grabbed the spare flashlight from her bag and moved into the trees.

Karin was completely silent now, even when Tessa called to her. Tessa pushed through the thick bushes until she reached the open parking lot. Two cars sat neatly at the tree's edge: Karin's and her own. A third car, small and pink, sat in the center of the clearing. *Fel's.*

Skid marks ran from behind its wheels. Tessa rounded

the vehicle to look in the front seat, and inhaled sharply. The windshield had been smashed. The safety glass hung together in fractured clumps, but a hole pierced it. Tessa cautiously stepped closer and angled her flashlight inside. Something dark stained the driver's seat.

"Fel!" Karin called from the trees behind her, and Tessa jumped away from the car.

She swung around, her heart hammering, and pointed her shaking flashlight toward the trees. She thought she saw a figure about thirty paces away; the pale skin was barely visible in the darkness. She began stumbling toward it. "Karin?"

Karin said something in reply, but Tessa was too far away to hear. She began moving faster, staggering through the brush and tripping over fallen trees, to reach the figure. Twenty paces away, she pulled up abruptly.

The person in the trees wasn't Karin—or Fel. It was far too tall and lean to be either of her companions.

She opened her mouth but couldn't find any words. Then the figure, without moving a muscle, said, "What is this?"

It was the most surreal experience of Tessa's life. The voice was Karin's, but the body wasn't. Tessa took a step backward, and the figure said, this time in Fel's voice, "Who are you? What are you doing?"

She took another step backward and bumped into something hard and cold. Tessa turned too quickly and lost her balance. She landed among the bracken in the woods' floor. Raising her head, she saw another of the shapes looming over her. It was taller than a human, and its skin was so pale, it almost glowed in the thin patches of moonlight that reached through the trees. Then Tessa caught sight of its face, and a scream boiled up inside her.

It had no eyes or nose. The skin stretched smoothly from its tangled hair until it reached the lips, thin and blue, that framed the mouth. Its teeth were blackened and pointed, sharp enough to tear cleanly through flesh.

The figure's lips opened. "What is this?" it said, imitating Karin's voice perfectly, as more of its companions melted out of the shadows to surround Tessa. "What is this?"

MUSIC BOX

Jackdaw, Jackdaw, how pretty you sing.
We'll visit the duke, we'll visit the king.

COLETTE OPENED HER EYES. HER WINDOW'S CURTAINS FLUTTERED
in the cool night air, allowing thin slices of moonlight to slink
across her bed. It had been a long time since she'd last dreamed
of the nursery rhyme she'd been forbidden to sing. *It must be at*
least ten years now since I last heard it.

Colette sat up in bed and ran her fingers through her hair to
untangle it. She couldn't remember what she'd been dreaming
about, but the song had been clear enough.

"Jackdaw, Jackdaw, how pretty you sing," she whispered to
herself. She couldn't remember beyond the first two lines, though
she'd once had the entire song memorized.

In the decade since she'd last heard it, Colette had almost

forgotten the drama surrounding the tune. The dream had brought it all back, though the events were hazy and out of order. She dug her thumbs into the corners of her eyes as she struggled to remember.

She found the little music box on the front porch while letting her cat out before school. It was a small round container, the type that opened up when its key was twisted and had a tiny ballerina twirling on one leg. Colette wanted to know who had left it so she could thank them. Her mother guessed it was a friend or a neighbor.

Colette played with the box for a solid hour that afternoon, reciting the tinkling song. *Jackdaw, Jackdaw, how pretty you sing. We'll visit the duke, we'll visit the king.* At bedtime, she'd put it into her toy chest, carefully nestled among the stuffed bears and the worn building blocks.

She woke in the early hours of the morning to find the box on her dressing table, the little ballerina twirling as the eerie song echoed through the room. Her first thought was that her mother had put it there as a surprise. She turned it off, stuffed it inside her closet, and went back to bed.

The following morning, a large black bird had hopped after her while she walked to school. Throughout the day, any time she looked out the classroom windows, she caught sight of the creature perched in a nearby tree.

Collette didn't touch the music box that evening but left it in the bottom of her closet. When it woke her, she was irritable enough to carry it to her mother's room. "Stop turning it on," she demanded, slamming the box onto the small bedside table as her mother sat up groggily. "I want to sleep!"

The following day, three black birds cawed to her as she walked through the park. Another five hovered in the parking lot when she left school.

For a third night running, the mournful tune woke her shortly after two in the morning. The box stood open on her dresser, the ballerina spinning tirelessly. When Colette took it to her mother, demanding an explanation, her mother retorted with questions of her own. Had Colette taken it out of the garbage? How had she known it had been thrown away? It didn't take long for the line of questioning to change. Had Colette been talking to strangers? Did she let anyone into the house? The night ended with Colette's mother taking the music box to the pond two streets down from their house and throwing it in.

That morning, when Colette opened the door to go to school, she found her front lawn filled with black birds. They fluttered and cawed as they saw her. Sitting on the front porch was the music box. It popped open as she looked at it, and the tinny tune surrounded her. *Jackdaw, Jackdaw, how pretty you sing. We'll visit the duke, we'll visit the king.*

She wasn't allowed to go to school that day. Instead, she and her mother stayed indoors and watched the music box burn in the fireplace. That had been the last of the song and the last of the black birds. Colette had been forbidden from repeating the tune, and gradually, the memories had faded.

Colette sat with her knees pulled up in front of her chest, just like she had that day. The memory had been so lost that it felt like digging a time capsule out of her mind. True to her promise, she had not sung the song since the music box had been burned.

Three brief, twanging notes cut through the silent night. Colette drew a breath and turned toward the window. A small twirling silhouette was visible behind the gauzy curtains.

Slowly, cautiously, she moved toward it and pulled the fabric aside. The music box waited on her windowsill, charred and partially melted. The ballerina's sweet face had been distorted so that she looked as though she were screaming. Her raised leg was bent at an odd angle, but she continued to move in small, sharp jerks as the song twanged out of the long-dormant player.

Colette raised her eyes toward the trees outside her window. Hundreds of beady eyes stared back. One of the birds shuffled, and its movement spurred the others into motion until the swarm of black creatures were flapping, cawing, and cackling at her.

She took a step back from the window. The birds swooped. They moved as one mass, pouring through the open window, enveloping her, and muffling her scream.

In an instant, the room was emptied. All that was left behind was a scattering of black feathers and the charred music box that continued to play its broken song.

Jackdaw, Jackdaw, how pretty you sing.
We'll visit the duke, we'll visit the king.
Jackdaw, Jackdaw, sing over my bed,
But break my sleep, and I'll wake up dead.

GHOST TOWN

"HERE SHE IS." GARY SLOWED THE VAN TO A CRAWL AS IT ENTERED the cluster of buildings that comprised Preyor Town. He leaned forward, straining his bulk against the seat belt, to get a better look at the stone and wood houses. "So this is what a ghost town looks like."

Beth was huddled deep into her seat, as though pulling back could physically move her away from the deserted buildings. She glared at the dashboard resolutely. "Great. You've seen it. Let's move on."

"Not just yet," Gary said in the most placating tone he could manage.

Beth shot him a glare.

"We've taken a two-hour detour to get here. We may as well enjoy it."

"Two hours?" Beth gasped. "I only agreed because you said it was virtually on our path!"

"Ehhh." Gary pulled up in the middle of the town and parked the car. "Yes, well, either way, it would be a damn shame not to have a poke around."

"I swear." Beth's voice was dangerously low. "If this makes us late for Sarah's christening…"

"Course it won't, love." Gary risked giving his wife's cheek a peck then opened the door and got out. The streets, filled with dust and long-dead weeds, stretched away to either side. He rubbed his hands together and moved toward one of the closer buildings, which he guessed must have been either a large house or a small hotel.

The door opened without protest. Inside was cool and dark, and the air smelled faintly mildewy. Gary paused in the foyer to appreciate the wooden ceiling and stained plaster on the walls. Like many pioneering towns, Preyor had been built in a rush, and it showed. The rough-hewn wood was mostly unpainted, and the carpet was shabby.

Gary moved deeper into the building, glancing through doorways and trying to guess the rooms' purposes. Much of the furniture had been taken, but larger fixtures such as the desks and shelves had been left behind. It wasn't until he pushed into a particularly large room and saw a saloon's bar against one wall that he realized it must have been the town's hotel. Gary approached the bar and wiped a finger through the thick reddish dust blanketing it, then he turned quickly as a chuckle from somewhere deeper in the building disturbed him. It had sounded like a child, but the noise had been so faint that Gary wasn't entirely sure he'd even heard it.

Probably another holidaying family stopping off. Gary returned to the foyer. A staircase rose to his right, the fabric on the steps well-worn and faded. Gary cast a final glance toward the front doors, where he knew his irritable wife would be waiting with the car, then hurried up the stairs. *She won't mind another minute or two.*

Halfway to the second floor, Gary froze. He'd heard it again: children's voices, too faint to make out their words. Only this time, they'd come from the upstairs rooms…

The stairs opened onto a long, narrow hallway. To the left, a window overlooked the main street. He could see Beth, forced out of the car by the heat, leaning on their van's hood. She still had her arms crossed, and he could picture her chewing at her lip like she did every time things didn't go her way.

He turned back to the hallway and tried the first door. It opened into a classic hotel room and, to his surprise, much of the furniture was still intact. The bed, the mattress, and even the bedside table were still in place. *If someone wanted to come in here and haul away the furniture, they could make a small fortune pawning it at a secondhand store.*

Laughter echoed through the hallway, and Gary swiveled as the shock sent his heart rate up. The sounds were closer than they had been before. One of the children seemed to be singing. Gary tried to make out the tune, but he didn't recognize it.

Suddenly uncomfortable in the deserted hotel, Gary moved back into the hallway. He glanced in each direction, and saw a flash of motion at the end of the hallway. There was a small gap between the door and its frame, and someone had darted past it.

"Hello?"

The giggles intensified, and Gary felt a flush of frustration. *Their parents shouldn't be letting them run around unsupervised like this. Where* are *their parents, anyway? I didn't see any other cars in the street.*

Against his better judgment, Gary edged toward the final room. The children whispered to each other then paused to giggle. Something was not quite right about their laughter, though. Earlier, it had been merry and bright, but the newer giggles had a malicious edge to them. *Like the way children laugh when they pull an insect's wings off.*

Gary stretched out a hand and nudged open the door. The hinges groaned as the wooden board moved inward. The room was completely empty, except for the marks of small bare feet in the dust on the floor.

Gary licked at his dry lips as he edged into the room. "Hello?"

The voices had fallen silent. Gary looked about, but there was nowhere to hide in the vacant space. *Unless they got out through the window...*

He approached the frame. The room was on the second floor, and he couldn't see any way for a child—let alone multiple children—to get out without making a lot of noise.

The window overlooked the main stretch of road, and Gary saw his car waiting below. The dark-green paint stood out starkly against the red soil. Beth was no longer leaning against the hood. Gary bent forward to rest his head against the cold glass and squinted. His wife wasn't inside the car, either. Gary's insides turned cold. He knew his wife too well to think she had wandered after him or gone to explore on her own.

The door behind him slammed, and Gary jumped. Raucous, malicious giggles came from the other side of the door, accompanied by the patter of running feet.

"Hey," Gary yelled, lurching toward the door. "Hey, what the hell?"

He grasped the handle and tugged on it, but it wouldn't budge. He pulled and pushed. Then he shoved his shoulder into the door to no avail. He tried not to scream as a child's hand, icy cold, fastened around his neck.

MAGPIE GIRL

HENRY LAY ON HIS BACK, HIS EYES FIXED ON THE SHADOWS SLINK-
ing across the ceiling. It was one of the nights where he found it
impossible to sleep.

Far below his apartment window, a car horn blared. Sirens
wailed in the distance. Two men, their words slurred, were
arguing. By the sounds of it, at least one of them would end up
in the hospital.

There was once a time when Henry would have cared. He'd
gone into the police force with great expectations for himself and
his career. *I won't be like the others*, he'd told himself. *I won't go
crooked. Every move, every action, will be for the benefit of this city
I love.*

If it had been any other sort of night, he might have laughed at
his own naivety. Instead, all he could do was watch the shadows,
which looked so much like a woman's fingers.

He'd made mistakes along his path, of course. Laziness had gotten the better of him on a few occasions and delayed justice. He'd accepted a couple of bribes. Looking back on it, he was almost certain he'd sent an innocent man to jail. But his worst offense—the mistake that haunted him into his old age—was the Magpie Girl.

He'd been on shift when she'd come into the station. One glance at her was all he needed to make an assessment. Her hoodie was old and stained. She wore leggings, even though it was winter. Her hair, bleached blond with the brown roots showing, had been dragged into a messy bun on the top of her head. The way she held herself—slouched, her shoulders hunched and head down—and the dark circles around her eyes had earned her a damning label: druggie.

At the time, Henry had been proud of himself for listening patiently to her story. He'd heard some wild stuff in his days, but hers had taken the cake. Her boyfriend was into occult stuff, she said. "He owns a heap of those old books with weird symbols on their covers," she'd said. "He's building up to something bad… trying to trap a soul to its body."

Henry had idly wondered what she was on. One of the psychedelic drugs, he'd assumed at first, but her focus and intensity made him lean more toward coke or possibly even an experimental custom brew.

Her story had gradually grown wilder, and Henry had been too fascinated to stop her. She claimed her boyfriend was a serial killer, on top of being into the occult.

"He's been taking prostitutes," she'd said, speaking rapidly. "He's experimenting on them. It never works, of course, but he keeps trying. When they die, he bags them and hides them in our apartment wall. There've been so many of them. At least twelve in the last year."

"Does he space them out to one a month," Henry had asked, "or did he blow through his budget in a few weeks?"

It had been a joke. A stupid, cruel, horrible joke. If Henry were capable of going back in time, he would have slapped himself.

A range of expressions crossed the woman's face. Henry had glimpsed confusion, then shock, then hurt that was quickly hidden behind outrage.

"You're supposed to help," she spat, pulling back from the desk.

"I can help you get into rehab," Henry had said, unable to keep the laughter out of his voice.

As she'd stormed out of the station, one of Henry's coworkers gave him a look that clearly said, "Did you have to go that far?"

Subconsciously, Henry had known he'd crossed a line. He even felt a twinge of shame as the station's door slammed. But other matters had pulled on his attention, and the mysterious woman was all but forgotten by the end of the day.

He'd thought he would never see her again. As he lay in his room, watching the shadows at two in the morning, as far from sleep as it was possible for a human to be, Henry would have given anything to have been right.

A week later, he'd responded to reports of a homicide in one of the worse parts of the city. He recognized the girl immediately. Her eyes were a little more sunken, and the dark hair roots a couple inches farther advanced than he remembered, but the face was familiar. The rest of her was borderline unrecognizable.

She'd been laid out in the center of the shabby room, her blood seeping into the cheap gray carpet, her hair spread in a halo about her head. Her killer had sliced her open with surgical precision and peeled strips of her skin back, laying it out beside her like an animal-hide rug. Henry couldn't even fathom what had been done to her. Candles had been placed on exposed rib bones. Ink ran between her intestines, and a congealed mess of something that pathology had later identified as chicken blood was mixed in. Henry's partner had fled from the room to retch in the hallway.

The shock had lasted for a long time. No one else seemed to remember the girl's visit to the police station, and Henry, terrified of what the repercussions could be if his negligence made it into the papers, kept his lips sealed.

He'd tried to remember as much of the bizarre discussion as he could, but it only came back in fragments. One part that had stuck with him was the imagery of a multitude of bodies bagged and stored in the walls. He'd nonchalantly instructed some junior officers to search behind the plaster for possible hidden weapons—and, sure enough, a cascade of decaying, ghost-white, plastic-shrouded bodies tumbled from behind a fake wall.

A suspect was apprehended. The trial dragged on for years. Every time he was called up to give testimony, Henry had wanted to tell them how the girl had come to see him just a week before her death and told him about her serial-killing, occult-obsessed boyfriend. But every time, a sense of self-preservation had stilled his tongue, and he stuck to his official alibi—that the first he knew of the business was the day he'd arrived at the apartment.

A combination of wormy lawyers and a lack of evidence saw the suspect go free. As far as the state was concerned, it was an unsolved case; the police were still working on it, picking up tips as they came in and hoping to get lucky, but there wasn't much hope of a resolution. The killer had been perfectly methodical with his butchering. If he'd left DNA, it hadn't been found. The apartment had been rented under a fake name, and no one knew much of anything about the occupants, who'd arrived and left in the early hours of the morning. They never even figured out the girl's real name. The media had named her after the apartment block: the Magpie Girl.

Henry didn't have any doubts about the killer's identity, though. He'd seen the way the boy had smirked when the nonguilty verdict was handed down. He wondered if the man was still free, possibly living in another part of the country under an assumed name, possibly carrying out more of his bizarre and morbid experiments. Henry had resigned himself to the idea that he would probably never hear the full story.

The shadows across the ceiling, so much like women's fingers, twitched and quivered. They began dragging themselves across the plaster, toward Henry's door. He always shut the door when he went to bed, but it always somehow ended up open at that terrible hour of three in the morning. The shadows slid down the walls and collected in a pool on the ground. Then came the noises: the scraping, dragging sounds that echoed unnaturally through the room. The gurgle of a breath being pulled through damaged lungs. The rasp of flesh being dragged across carpet.

Henry turned his head toward the doorway, where a dark shape was dragging itself into his room. "Leave me alone," he begged for what felt like the hundredth time. "I'm *sorry*. Leave me alone."

The corpse raised its head, as it always did, and Henry caught a glimpse of her body, sliced open, the flaps of skin dragging across the carpet. Her eyes, cold and dead, fixed on the retired policeman, and the Magpie Girl stretched a hand forward to drag herself closer to her victim.

HAZARD LIGHTS

MARIA LEANED AGAINST THE CAR DOOR AND STARED THROUGH the window at the harsh white lights spaced along the Lane Cove Tunnel. The driver kept trying to start a conversation, but she'd caught a red-eye flight and was beyond exhausted. All she wanted to do was get to her hotel and sleep for a lifetime.

The traffic wasn't cooperating, though. It had been gridlocked for the last twenty minutes, and in the tunnel, it seemed even worse. Maria didn't think they'd moved more than ten meters in the last five minutes.

"Bad traffic today, yeah?" The taxi driver, a cheerful man with a thick black beard beamed at her in the rear-vision mirror, and Maria mustered a thin smile.

"Uh-huh."

"Haven't seen it this bad in months. Must be a breakdown ahead."

"Hmm." Maria turned to look out of the opposite window, where she could see five other car lanes—two more going in their direction, the other three going the opposite—all forced to a halt. Every now and then, a car would crawl a few inches closer to its leader, as though that would make any sort of difference.

The radio came to life with a crackle, and Maria jumped. She'd nearly fallen asleep.

"We are currently experiencing an emergency situation," the voice on the radio said, and Maria leaned forward to listen to it. Her driver hadn't touched the radio, she knew, by the way his face had gone pale; however, because the tunnel dipped below ground to carry cars from one side of the harbor to the other, the control room had the ability to activate the car's radios in an emergency.

"Remain in your vehicle," the voice said. He sounded flustered and panicky, though he was clearly reading from a script. "Extinguish all lights and remain silent. Assistance will be sent as soon as possible."

The radio fell silent. Maria looked to her taxi driver, whose face had lost almost all color. He turned the key in the ignition, powering the car down and killing its lights. Around her, other cars were also being turned off.

Maria swiveled in her seat to look behind her. She thought she could hear noises coming from deeper in the tunnel. Then the multitude of lights spaced along the concrete walls whined and died, plunging them into darkness.

Someone shrieked, and car doors slammed. A handful of headlights were still on, and Maria tried to see what was happening through the limited glow, but everything was a mess of shadows and shapes.

The radio crackled for a second time, and the voice returned. Its panic had risen to a nearly hysterical pitch, and he didn't seem to be reading from a script any longer. "They say you should remain in your cars...but...but... They're still finding you... don't run. Don't bother. They'll catch you. They're spreading so fast. I've never seen or heard of anything like this before... Oh, jeez, I'm so, so sorry! Stay in your cars. Stay—"

The voice broke off with a gasp, and Maria heard a banging noise in the distance followed by what sounded like metal being twisted and torn. The radio clicked off.

Maria sat frozen in her seat as she stared at her driver. A car a few rows ahead turned on its hazard lights, and the flashing red reflected off the driver's face as he stared back.

Then the screams started.

Maria turned to look behind them and saw shapes—people— running between the cars. It was more than panic; it was pandemonium. Several figures shoved against her taxi as they ran past, making it sway. Maria placed one hand on the car door, preparing to exit and join the crowd, but she stopped when she caught sight of other, larger shapes farther back in the tunnel.

They were barely visible in the blinking hazard light, but they were definitely not human. The shapes moved on all fours, dexterously climbing over the cars and scuttling along the tunnel's walls. Their limbs had at least four joints each, and they were larger than an average man.

They snatched up the fleeing humans so quickly that the motions were a blur. Maria heard the crackles and snaps of breaking bones underneath the screams. Glass smashed as the creatures pounded through car windows.

"Get down!" the taxi driver hissed, shoving Maria out of her seat so that she was kneeling in the footwell. She flattened herself as much as she could, trying to breathe through her mouth to minimize the noise. The taxi driver sunk back into his seat, his eyes wide as he tried not to shake.

From her position, Maria could still see the figures racing past the windows and feel the impact as they bumped the car. Then the taxi shuddered as something large and heavy landed on it, and one of the running figures by her window was pulled from view with a gurgling shriek. Maria pressed her hand over her mouth and held her breath. They were enveloped by silence for a second, then there was a horrific crash as the windshield was broken by a long, tough limb.

The taxi driver barely managed half a scream before he was torn out of his seat and pulled through the hole in the windshield. His voice choked off, then, and dark liquid splashed across the window above Maria.

The sounds were changing as the screams faded into the distance. The human cacophony was replaced by steady, loud thuds as the creatures climbed over the cars, making snapping noises and chewing, tearing sounds. Maria squeezed her eyes closed so that she wouldn't have to watch the shadows move past the window.

She kept still until the noises died into the distance and were eventually entirely extinguished. Her muscles ached from the cramped position. Outside, the tunnel remained dark except for the hazard lights, which continued to bathe the area in intermittent flashes of red. She was surrounded in near-perfect silence—no footsteps, voices, thudding limbs, or tearing flesh.

Maria shook as she slowly, cautiously rose to her knees. She peeked through the car's window, between the streaks of blood, to see that the tunnel seemed empty. So did the cars. Their human occupants had been stripped from them, pulled through broken windows or holes that had been carved in the metal. Maria alone had been spared, thanks to her hiding place.

I've got to leave before those creatures come back. There should be emergency exits placed along the walls. They should be too small for those...things...to fit through easily. If I can just get to one of them...

Maria opened her door slowly and silently. The car's interior lights automatically turned on in response, and Maria looked out, frozen in terror, as a dozen pairs of reflective, globe-like eyes turned toward her.

THE RESIDENT

ALLIE SHIFTED THE CROWBAR TO HER LEFT HAND AS SHE GLANCED up and down the length of the plywood boards covering the space below her home. The crawlspace had been boarded up since before Allie bought the property. The real estate agent had said it would make an excellent storage space, though. And with another five months until the weather would be warm enough to work in her garden, Allie figured she might as well put the storage space to use and clear up her yard.

Allie approached one of the plywood boards and pressed the tip of her crowbar into the narrow gap above it. The wood had discolored from years of exposure to the weather, but it had held up surprisingly well. It groaned, creaked, and cracked as Allie forced the gap wider, then it broke free with a loud snap. She pulled the board away and threw it aside, leaving a two-foot opening into the crawlspace.

She dropped the crowbar and picked up the flashlight she'd set on the porch. Allie angled the harsh white beam into the space below. It was larger than she'd expected. While only a three-foot-high gap was visible from the outside, the ground dipped just past the entrance, creating nearly enough room for a person to stand upright.

It was hard to see with only a small circle of light, but there seemed to be items already stored in the space below her home. She saw something that looked like a broken chair, as well as a pile of bags nestled into the corner. The house's support pillars blocked much of her view, and Allie, with a final glance at the garden, lowered herself into the crawlspace.

It was a tight fit through the plywood hole, but just beyond, the ground dropped away, and she was able to move forward when she crouched.

The air was much cooler than outside. A smell—dirty, musty, and decayed—hung in the air. Allie pressed her sleeve over her nose to block out the stench and moved toward the plastic bags.

They were all sealed, but several had split down the side. They looked as though they were filled with garbage. *Did the previous owners seriously leave their trash down here?*

Allie poked at one of the split bags with her foot, and rags fell out. They looked as if they'd once been clothes, but had been worn down until holes developed and seams broke, making them unwearable. Under the clothes were broken plates and cups and bent cutlery.

A quiet scratching noise disturbed her, and Allie turned in time to see a rat scamper out of her flashlight beam to hide behind…

A mattress?

Allie approached the lumpy shape, trying to breathe through her mouth as much as possible. The mattress had broken down, and several of its springs poked through the fabric, but strangely enough, someone seemed to have patched it with rags similar to the ones in the bags. It was pressed against one of the support pillars, which had hid it from view of Allie's hole in the plywood.

Beyond the mattress, a handmade shelf stood propped against the wall. Allie moved toward it then jumped as her foot hit something, sending it clattering across the dirt. She turned the flashlight down and saw empty cans—dozens of them—littering the ground.

A voice in the back of Allie's head was telling her to get out—and get out fast—but curiosity compelled her toward the shelf.

She cast her light over the odd collection arranged on the wooden boards: a plate, a cup, a spoon, a fork, and a knife. Next to them sat two candle stubs, burned down to their bases.

On the shelf below stood a strange assortment of toys: a doll, too filthy for use, a pull toy that had lost almost all of its bright paint, and a coloring book propped upright as though it were an art display. Allie reached toward it gingerly and pulled the cover back. The pages inside had been colored so thoroughly and so vigorously that she couldn't see a single inch of white paper. It was almost as though its owner had been over the same pages dozens of times. Even so, the coloring was crude, and in many cases, the artist hadn't even tried to stay within the lines. The final item on the shelf was a Polaroid camera. It reminded Allie of the camera she'd inherited from her grandfather. She thought she still had it in storage somewhere, though she hadn't seen it in years.

Nausea was rising in Allie's stomach. She turned toward the crawlspace's exit—and froze. A series of Polaroid photos were stuck to the pillar beside the mattress. They were clumsy and often blurry, but it was impossible for Allie to mistake the subject.

The photos were of her. Some showed her digging in her yard—*that must have been months ago, when I planted the garden*—and others were of her leaving the house and locking the door behind herself. A final series, stuck in place of pride near the mattress's head, had been taken through her bedroom window and showed Allie asleep in her bed. In the closest photo, Allie wore the pajamas she'd purchased just a week previously.

Allie's hand rose to cover her mouth. She turned toward the square of light in the plywood wall, her escape, and inhaled sharply. A person—or something that resembled a person— stood in the light. His face sagged strangely, as though his body had been sucked dry. His eyes bugged out of his head with a terrific intensity. Limp hair ran down to frame his cheeks, which housed an unnaturally large mouth.

Then his mouth opened, splitting into a smile, as the batteries in Allie's light died.

HOST

KIRA MUTED HER TELEVISION AND FROWNED AT THE CALLER ID flashing on her phone. *Jessika Kirble.* She hadn't thought of Jessika in years, let alone heard from her.

She, Jessika, and Adelaide had been close friends in school. Just seeing her name brought up a myriad of memories: weekly sleepovers, fights over toys, and, as they'd gotten older, fights over boys. At the time, their bond had felt unbreakable.

Time had eroded the friendship, of course, as it did everything. When Kira's friends split up to go to different high schools, she'd found it surprisingly easy to move into new friendships and forget the old—and seemingly childish—camaraderie.

So how did Jessika get my number? And why's she calling me now, after more than ten years of silence? If she wants to recruit me to one of those pyramid scheme makeup parties, she can think again.

Kira pressed the green answer button and held the cell phone to her ear. "Hello?"

The voice on the other end let out a relieved breath. It sounded oddly scratchy and distant, but the tone was shockingly familiar. "Kira! Hey, it's Jessika. From school. D'you remember?"

"Yeah, of course!" Kira forced a note of brightness into her voice. It felt surreal to be talking to her childhood friend, as though she'd somehow stepped back in time. "How are you? Wow, it's been ages."

Jessika chuckled. "It sure has. I've been great. Though I've always felt bad that we didn't stay in touch. Do you think we could meet up?"

Maybe she does just want to reconnect, after all. "Yeah, I'd love that. Let me take you out for coffee."

"No, no, I mean tonight. Can you meet me tonight?"

Kira's subconscious prickled. Something about the urgent note in the other woman's voice was unsettling.

Jessika quickly added, "I know, I'm sorry. I wouldn't ask, except it's urgent. It's about Adelaide."

Adelaide Du. The third member of our miniature clique. She was heart-set on being a vet, wasn't she? "Is something wrong with her?" Kira sat forward on her couch. The muted television had moved on to a commercial break, and an enthusiastic woman was demonstrating how much liquid her mopping cloth could absorb.

"Uh..." Jessika was silent for a very long time. When she finally spoke, a fake brightness saturated her voice. "It's really something I need to talk to you about in person. Can you come? Tonight?"

The unsettling prickles evolved into an anxious buzz. "Where?"

"We could meet up in the parking lot by the convenience store on Mendle Street. In Reddington. Is that okay with you?"

At least it's a public place. Not that I don't trust her. I just…don't trust her. "That's fine. I'll be twenty minutes."

Kira almost never visited Reddington, and she had never been to the convenience store Jessika wanted to meet at. It wasn't a good part of town. Half of the shops she passed were closed, and the other half looked as though they were barely hanging on. Tape held together fractured windows on houses, or cardboard covered spaces where the windows had been completely broken. Kira hadn't seen a single other human on the streets she'd passed, though there seemed to be no shortage of stray animals. The streetlights that still functioned did an appalling job of lighting the grime-coated pathways.

Her uneasiness was growing with each turn she took. *Maybe Jessika's on drugs and is going to beg for money. Or just straight-up rob me.*

Those concerns weren't at all alleviated when Kira arrived at where the convenience store should have been and found a long-abandoned shell of a building. Part of the roof had collapsed. The only light came from the glow of streetlamps in the road that ran behind the store.

This is insane. I've got to get out of here.

As she coasted past the abandoned shop, she saw a figure

standing near the shopping cart corrals. Its pose was, in a strange way, incredibly familiar. The woman—*Jessika*—stepped forward and waved an arm in an attempt to attract Kira's attention.

I should go. This place doesn't bode well.

Jessika was waving both arms. She looked desperate.

Damn it.

Kira pulled into the parking lot and put on the handbrake, but she didn't remove the keys from the ignition. She got out of her car and carefully moved toward Jessika, who was waiting for her by the corral.

"Thanks for coming," Jessika said, beaming at her.

Kira hoped her shock wasn't too apparent. Her childhood friend had changed incredibly in ten years. She'd once been plump, with dimples in her cheeks and a bouncy kind of energy. That night, she seemed to be nothing except for bones. Her skin drooped heavily, and deep-gray shadows rimmed her eyes, which were bloodshot and slightly unfocused. Only the energy remained, and she was expressing it in strange tics and hand flutters.

"How've you been?" Kira asked, trying not to look as repulsed as she felt.

Jessika smiled, her pale lips stretching into a shape that looked more like muscle memory than genuine emotion. "Great. Absolutely great. You're looking well. That's good. They take so much out of you, you really don't want to be going into it when you're already weak."

"What?" Kira had begun backing up, trying to put more

distance between herself and the gaunt woman, but Jessika was pacing forward and closing whatever gaps Kira built.

"It's really important, though," Jessika said. The plastic smile had frozen across her face. "That's what they say, anyway. I don't really understand it. But then, they don't want me for my brainpower, y'know? They just need a *host*."

Kira, now desperate to leave, turned toward her car. A second woman stood in front of the open driver door. Her face was masked in shadows, but Kira thought, behind the sunken cheeks, hollow eyes, and bloodless lips, the bone structure was faintly familiar. "A...Ad..."

"Yes, that's Adelaide. She called me first. But now it's my turn to recruit a new host, and I chose *you*."

Kira turned back to her old friend and screamed. Jessika's face was distorting. Her jaw stretched horrifically wide, and something dark was moving at the back of her throat. Kira staggered backward, too horrified to look away as small, slimy black insects began crawling across Jessika's tongue. They looked nothing like any creature Kira had seen before. A multitude of twitching legs and large transparent wings extended from flat, shiny bodies. The wings fluttered open, and the insects took flight when they reached Jessika's lips. Kira turned to run, but two unexpectedly strong arms wrapped around her torso and pinned her in place.

"Open wide," Adelaide whispered. Kira could feel the other woman's sagging flesh pressing into her as the viselike arms squeezed. "It will only take a moment."

Then the small, wet insects began hitting Kira's face. Their scratching feet felt across her cheeks and dug at her lips. Kira couldn't stand it any longer. She screamed, and the creatures gladly took advantage of the invitation to enter their new host.

SNOWBOUND

THE SCREECH OF TIRES SHOOK JACQUES OUT OF HIS SLEEP. THE abrupt stop lurched him forward in the train's seat, and his newspaper flopped to the ground. He blinked a few times to wake himself up then looked out the window.

Snow had been falling steadily and blanketed the mountainous region in white. Far in the distance, the black foothills were barely visible in the twilight, and every few meters, a clump of weedy, straggly green trees poked through the snow.

The train wasn't supposed to stop until it reached its destination, Holburg, on the other side of the mountains. Jacques glanced around to see if he might have missed an announcement, but the train's other occupants seemed just as confused as he was. The two fashionable ladies a few seats behind him were talking quickly in a language he didn't recognize. The young man who'd been eyeing the fashionable ladies was glancing about the carriage as though someone might be able to explain the delay. The thick-set bearded man and his petite wife opposite Jacques were quiet, but they seemed just as puzzled.

"What's going on?" the young man asked. "Are we there already?"

"Not for another few hours," the bearded man replied. He rose from his seat with a sigh. "Let me check."

The carriage was silent during the few minutes that the bearded man was gone. When he returned, he only shrugged. "They say we're snowed in."

"Isn't this supposed to be a snow-proof train?" The young man sounded indignant. One of the fashionable ladies made a comment to her friend, and they both had to smother snickers.

"There's no such thing as a snow-proof train," Jacques said, shuffling his newspaper back into order and folding it on the seat beside himself. "This one is designed to make it through light and moderate snow, but will still be stymied by anything heavy."

"Still, though," the young man said, looking out the window, "it's not quite heavy, is it?"

Jacques had to agree. The snow was thick enough to blanket, but he thought he would still be able to walk through it reason-ably well. The train shouldn't have any problems, but of course, there were a multitude of inconveniences that might have stopped them, such as an avalanche, falling rocks, or even just tracks that had succumbed to the weather and broken apart.

One of the train's assistants burst through the door at the back of the carriage and dashed down the aisle. The young man tried to call to him, but the assistant didn't stop. Jacques had a brief impression of a blanched-white face and bulging eyes before the man was past him, the air displaced by his motion, ruffling the newspaper. Then he was through the door at the other end of the carriage, presumably moving toward the train's engine.

The young man was demanding explanations again, even though it was clear that no one in the carriage knew any more than he did. Jacques tuned him out as he stared through the window at the softly drifting snow. He shifted forward in his seat and frowned. Despite the strength of the moon, the patchy trees and high mountains left most of the surrounding terrain in shadows. Jacques thought, though, that he'd seen a shape moving through the woods, just beyond the square of light coming from his window. *A person or a wolf...?*

A voice came through the train's intercom, sounding hurried and terse. "Apologies for this brief delay," it said at the same time as the train gave a jolt and began moving in reverse. "We have encountered unexpected obstacles and are required to return to Laksview for tonight."

"What?" The young man rose out of his seat. "That's a full two hours away!"

"Hush," the thickset man said. Jacques noticed he was squeezing his wife's hand. "I'm certain they have a good reason."

"But I have a hotel booked!"

Jacques didn't interrupt, but a prickling worry dug at him. He remembered his mother telling him stories about the mountains and the snow beasts that hid in their caves. *Fairy tales, of course. But still...*

The train was gradually picking up speed, slinking along the track, away from the narrow mountain pass it had been trying to move through. Jacques had barely relaxed in his seat when it gave another jolt.

"What now?" the young man snapped, but everyone else in the carriage froze. The motion hadn't been anything remotely like the way a train was supposed to move. It was a harsh jerk in the wrong direction, as though something monumentally large were pulling the train to a halt.

Then the sound of screaming metal filled the carriage, making the fashionable women clasp their hands over their ears. The young man, the bearded man, and Jacques pulled their windows open and leaned their torsos as far out of the train as they dared.

Jacques looked toward the front carriage, but the night and flurries obscured the view. He thought, however, that the carriage seemed to be tilting upward...

"Run!" the bearded man cried, pushing his wife out of her seat and dragging her toward the carriage's rear door. "It has the train. Stop looking! Run!"

Everything was motion. Jacques pushed out of his chair and joined the others running to the carriage's door as the sounds of screams from farther up in the train reached him. He followed the fashionable ladies outside, into the icy mountains. The frozen wind bit at his face, but he didn't dare go back for his luggage. In the distance, he saw the outline of a beast silhouetted against the starry sky, impossibly large, lifting the first carriage clear off its tracks and raising it like a child picking up a toy.

Jacques didn't dare look back again, but focused on the ground ahead of him. He heard more carriage doors slam, followed by the screams of their occupants fleeing the shuddering, jerking train. He tried to stay with the group, knowing that survival together was more likely than survival alone, and only realized his error as the forerunner, the young man, screamed. A dark shape had darted out of the shadows and thrown him to the ground. Two more followed it quickly, sinking black teeth into the man's limbs as he fought for his life.

It was nearly impossible for Jacques to peel his eyes away, but when he did, he saw more of the black creatures—*parasites,* his mind told him; *they're parasitic creatures picking off the prey brought down by an apex predator*—materializing out of the shadows and bringing down the fleeing men and women.

Jacques froze, unsure of what to do. Should he return to the carriage—that might afford safety from the black creatures but make him vulnerable to the gigantic, hulking monster that blotted out the moon—or continue with his companions and hope for the best?

He never had a chance to make up his mind—the next moment, three sets of razor-sharp teeth sank into his back.

RED OAK HOUSE

MARCH PARKED HIS CAR IN THE WEEDY DRIVEWAY AND DIMMED its lights. The house, three stories tall and built from time-stained wood, stood like a sentry on the slope. He admired it for a moment before picking his notebook, pen, and camera off the seat beside him and slipping out of the car.

This'll be the last one, he told himself for the fiftieth time that day. *The last one, then the book's off to the editor. And, provided I picked the right house, it'll be the best out of all of them.*

For the past three years, March had spent his weekends and evenings researching haunted locations in the Summerset area. The region was supposedly a hotspot for the paranormal; civil war battle sites, a mass grave, and the state's largest disused asylum created fertile grounds for spiritual unrest.

March's research had been meticulous. Every fact was verified and each experience documented as thoroughly as possible. He'd spoken to all of the area's ghost hunters, both hobbyists and professionals. And one very interesting interview had led him to the Red Oak House.

While there had never been a verifiable ghost sighting in the building—the stories amounted to a friend of a friend's account, of which there were versions for almost every old house in the country—the Red Oak House did have an exceptionally dark history. The Gable family had built it in the eighteenth century. Their eldest son had been considered odd, but no one had ever questioned his sanity until he butchered his entire family and buried their remains in the garden behind the house.

The massacre went undiscovered for weeks. When the town realized his crime, the villagers had gathered as a mob to storm the home. But the son, rather than let the mob kill him, had hung himself from a window before they could reach him. From then on, every single family who had occupied the house had suffered tragedy.

March tried the house's front door first, but it was boarded closed. He glanced behind himself, to where the empty, moonlit rural road stretched in each direction, then he slunk around the house's side to check the windows and back door.

It was technically a private property, which meant he was breaking and entering, but no one had lived in the house in more than two decades. March suspected the building's owner probably wouldn't have minded if it was burned to the ground.

The Messenger family had moved in following the Gables' deaths. Within a year of occupancy, the father choked to death on a fish bone. Barely two months afterward, the eldest son was kicked in the head by a horse and died in the hospital. When the youngest child drowned in the river behind the house, Mrs. Messenger had taken her two remaining children and fled the home.

The back door was also boarded over, but the window beside it was missing its glass. Using his jacket's sleeves as protection, March hoisted himself over the sill and dropped into the kitchen. The room looked almost perfectly intact. A layer of grime seemed to coat every surface, and dead leaves and insects were scattered over the wood floor. Pots still hung on their hooks above the range, and when he opened the fridge's door, March found it full of long-rotted food. He took a few steps back and photographed the room.

After the Messenger family, a young couple, the Stalleys, had taken up residence. Heavily pregnant, Mrs. Stalley had been attempting to draw water from the well behind the house when she'd stumbled and fallen into it. Her husband didn't hear her screams, and only discovered her body hours later. He'd been so grieved that he'd turned the shotgun from the mantel on himself.

March followed the kitchen through to the living room. The furniture sat where it had been left for two decades; the fabric was slowly rotting in the humid air. March examined the paintings on the wall then took several photos of the room before continuing to the staircase.

The house had remained empty for nearly five years following the Stalleys' deaths and was then occupied by the Volkers, an immigrant family. The youngest child swallowed lye. His sibling fell from the third-floor window. Mrs. Volkers overdosed on her medication. Mr. Volkers was run over by his own truck when he forgot to use the handbrake. All within the span of two years.

The stairs groaned under March's weight as he climbed them. The air tasted stagnant and sour, tainted by the decay of rooms that desperately needed tending.

The second-to-last family, the Smythes, left immediately after the death of their nephew, who'd been staying with them. He'd fallen into the threshing machine while it was running.

March turned left at the top of the stairs and began exploring and photographing each room he passed. There was a vast amount of history buried in them; he found a diary, which he pocketed, and several photo albums from the last occupant.

Carrie Jacobsen was the only single person to purchase the house, and she was the only resident whose death hadn't been confirmed. She'd lived there for six months then abruptly gone missing. While rumors circulated about possible grisly deaths, her neighbors believed she'd seen something supernatural and fled. The day before her disappearance, she'd mentioned hearing strange noises at night and feeling uncomfortable in her home.

If she'd left, she'd done so in a hurry. Her clothes were in the closets, eaten to shreds by moths and age. The police reports said her dinner plate was still soaking in the sink when the search parties combed the house looking for her.

March opened the door to the final room, Carrie's bedroom. It was neat, but dusty. He took two photos then began methodically opening the closets and searching for any details that could enrich his book. In one corner was a small frame set into the wall, holding a wooden door. March opened the door and glanced inside. It was a dumbwaiter; when the house was first built, the narrow chutes were common, used to carry food to the upper levels. March pointed his flashlight down the hole and said very quietly, "Oh."

At the bottom of the chute, where the box would have normally been, lay a pile of cloth. In among the cloth peeked little slivers of white bone.

March drew back, his mouth dry, as the shock of his discovery battled with morbid excitement. The house had claimed Carrie after all. Somehow, she'd fallen into the chute. *Did she die on impact, or was she still alive when her neighbors searched her house the following day?*

March took a step backward and raised the flashlight to photograph the chute. He was a second too late to hear the rotten wood cracking under his feet, as the house, long starved, claimed another victim.

OVERHEARD

"HE-E-EY," KYLIE SAID, FLIPPING BACKWARD ONTO THE COUCH and kicking off her sneakers. She noticed she had a hole in one sock, and wiggled the exposed toe.

"Hey yourself," Sarah said from the other end of the phone. "I miss you already, girl."

Kylie laughed as she stared at the decorative plaster bordering the ceiling. It was fancy. *Too* fancy, she'd decided, as though the house were trying to seem classier than a rural farmhouse had any right to be. "Nowhere near as much as I miss you. And Jem. And Tammy. I swear I'm going to die of boredom before this week's up."

"Ugh." Kylie could imagine her best friend rolling her eyes as she twisted the phone's cord around her fingers. "Then come back. It's not as if the house is going to die if it's left alone for too long."

Kylie groaned. "Mum says it's going to *build character*. I think she's hoping I'll turn into a country bumpkin while I'm here. Plus, she says we still owe the Joneses for that time they looked after our dog."

"Uh-huh."

"But there's literally nothing to do here. It's, like, an hour to walk to the shops, and there's nothing there except ugly fashion and a really nasty convenience store." Kylie rolled onto her side to look at the lounge room. She wasn't sure if the house needed new bulbs or if it had been built by an idiot, but the building never seemed bright enough, no matter how many lights she turned on. As soon as evening hit, the shadows clustered in and dimmed the room until she struggled to make out details in the corners and behind the multitude of bookcases.

"Hey, there's got to be something fun to do there." A teasing note had crept into Sarah's voice. "Feeding chickens. Sitting in a rocking chair for hours on end. *Sewing*."

"Shut up." Kylie made a face, even though her friend couldn't see her. Sarah laughed. In the moment of silence that followed, Kylie thought she detected a noise in the background of the phone. *What is that? Breathing?*

"Hey, did you hear that?" she asked. The noise was interrupted by what sounded like a fridge door opening and rustling as Sarah looked inside.

"Hear what?"

"Like, exhaling."

"Yeah, I do that sometimes." A container thudded onto a counter, and a lid was pulled off with a pop.

She's into the ice cream, then. Her parents can't be home.

"Yeah, but this sounded really…never mind. Has Travis said anything about me?"

"Forget him," Sarah said, her voice muffled as she filled her mouth with ice cream. "He's not worth your time, girl."

Kylie didn't reply. In the few seconds of dead air, she heard the breathing again. *That can't be Sarah. You can't breathe like that with your mouth full.*

"Hey, did you—"

"Yeah, I heard it that time," Sarah said, sounding annoyed. "That'll be the brat listening in on our call again. Tyler, get the hell off the phone!"

An exhale filled the pause in their conversation, and Kylie sat up on the couch, suddenly feeling cold. It had sounded… *sick* somehow, as though the person were breathing through a damaged larynx. She'd heard the sound before, years ago, when her grandmother was dying of throat cancer. She would have been happy to never hear it again.

"Tyler!" Sarah repeated, sounding angry. "I swear I'll beat your ass for this. Get off the damn phone."

The inhale, this time, was sticky and rattling. Kylie wrapped her arms around her torso. "Sarah, are you sure—"

"Hang on. Let me go punch some sense into the brat," Sarah said. "He must be using Mum's bedroom phone. Be back in a tic."

Kylie heard a click as Sarah placed the receiver on the kitchen counter, then her friend's footsteps thundered in the distance, accompanied by her yelling, "This is why everyone hates you, you ass."

Kylie let her eyes rove across the room as she waited. The shadows seemed to be thickening, as though they were seeping out of their corners and bleeding across the room. She had the distinct impression that, if she waited long enough, the darkness would swallow her. She closed her eyes and tapped her feet together, suddenly keen to hear her friend on the phone again.

Instead, the rasping, rattling breath returned, followed by a voice. It was a sound Kylie knew she'd never forget: cracked and somehow bubbling, as though the sounds had been drawn through a mangled neck. Despite that, the voice seemed pleased with itself, almost taunting.

"Hello, Kylie," it said, accompanied by another rattling breath. "You left the back door unlocked."

Kylie's mouth opened, though she didn't make a sound. The receiver clicked as the caller placed it back in its cradle. Two beats passed, then Sarah picked up her phone again, sounding breathless. "It wasn't Tyler," she said. "He's downstairs, playing video games with his friend."

The receiver dropped from Kylie's hands as the door behind her opened.

AN EMPTY CHURCH

"What do you think it is?" Clara asked, then corrected herself. "*Was.*"

"Church." Sam nodded toward the cross adorning the steeply slanted roof. "Must be old, though. I didn't think anyone lived near here."

Clara turned to glance at the trees behind them. They'd been crossing from the town to Sam's house, using the Potts Forest as a shortcut, when they'd become lost. Not that being lost in Potts Forest was dangerous; the woods were crisscrossed with hiking trails and roads. All the friends needed to do was keep walking until they came across a pathway then follow it back to town. Neither of them had been expecting to find signs of habitation in the forest, though.

"Want to look inside?" Sam grinned, and her braces reflected in the low afternoon light.

Clara sighed. "Really?"

"C'mon, yeah. Let's see what's left inside."

The church wasn't large. It was smaller than Clara's house, even. Sam was first to the door, and she pushed it open then wiped her hands on her jeans. "It's slimy."

"Wood's rotting," Clara noted. "Better be careful in there."

Sam made a mocking noise. "It's not *that* derelict. C'mon."

Inside, the church was so dim that Clara had to squint to make out the shapes. Rows of ancient, carved wooden pews faced the front of the church, where a simple pulpit stood below a stained-glass window. Clara blinked at the image in the glass, but it didn't seem to be any sort of religious scene. It showed a gigantic snake coiled in on itself, its mouth swallowing its tail so that it became a circle. The serpent's teeth pierced its own scales, sending rivulets of blood onto the black ground below it. Clara shuddered and turned away.

A communion table stood at the front of the church, its once-white crocheted cloth discolored and tatty from age. Clara approached the table and looked over the ornaments. There were no communion cups or baskets for bread. Instead, a range of ornate, twisting knives were laid out on the stained cloth, and a large bowl stood in the center of the table. The bowl's contents had dried during the decades the church had been forgotten, but it had left a black sediment in the base. Clara found herself imagining a congregation lining up to slice their hands and mingle their blood in the bowl. She forced herself to look away. *This place is too weird.*

"Sam? Ready to go?" Clara hoped she'd kept the anxiety out of her voice, but she couldn't stop it thundering through her veins as she looked about the room and saw she was alone. "Sam?"

No answer.

Clara crossed her hands over her chest and tried to slow her breathing. She moved to the center of the church and looked up and down the rows of pews. A door—one she couldn't remember seeing before—stood open below the stained-glass window. Clara squinted at it. She thought she could hear faint noises coming from the darkness: halting, stumbling footsteps, and shoes scraping across the stone floor.

Clara reluctantly approached the door and held her breath to listen to the sounds. The footsteps mingled with a voice, but the sound was too low for her to understand what it was saying. She glanced down and saw the dust had been wiped off the door handle. Someone had gone that way recently.

Clara cleared her throat, but her voice still came out as a whisper. "Sam?"

"Yes, Clara?" Sam's voice, placid, came from inside the doorway.

"Sam, get out of there. I want to go."

Silence. Clara leaned into the doorway, hoping to see her companion. The faint light from the church's entrance and the holes in the roof couldn't illuminate more than the first few steps, but she could see a stone stairwell leading downward. *Does the church have a basement?*

"Sam?" Clara called again, but there was still no response.

Clara steeled herself then stepped over the threshold and into the stairwell.

Almost immediately, the darkness engulfed her, making her feel cloistered and smothered. She tried to draw breath, but it felt like inhaling water. She tried to call, but her voice stuck in her throat. Moving her feet felt like dragging her limbs through mud, but she moved forward slowly and deliberately as the blackness pressed in on her from all sides.

Panic rose through her chest as she tried to call again and found her voice choked. She turned back to find the door, but all was darkness. She couldn't see the light, she couldn't see the door, and she couldn't see Sam. She tried to scream, but the sound was doused before it could even reach her own ears.

I'm suffocating. Even though she was still dragging breaths into her lungs, it felt nothing like any sort of air she'd inhaled before. Dead and heavy, it made her want to retch. She flung herself forward, toward where she thought the door had been, but her fingers grazed only the air. Her feet slipped out from under her as she fell forward. She braced herself to hit the floor, but instead, she slammed into the door, upright.

Clara took a stumbling half step back, but didn't dare take her fingers away from the doorframe. She scrabbled over it, searching for the handle—and a way out—as she fought to inhale the toxic substance that threatened to drown her. A choking sob escaped her raw throat, but the sound was perfectly smothered. She couldn't hear a thing, not her heartbeat, not the sounds of her fingernails splintering as she clawed at the door with increased desperation, and not the sounds of her hungry, futile gasps. Then the door swung open on its own, and Clara stumbled through it.

She was back in the forest, facing the path she and Sam had been following. She drew a sharp, gasping breath, relieved to feel real air in her lungs again. When she turned, she found the church just behind her, its front door wide open.

That's impossible. She rotated to see the forest again and caught sight of a figure near the edge of the trees. She recognized the jeans and slightly too-large sweater and stumbled toward her friend. "Sam?"

Sam turned slowly. Her face was sheet-white and coated with sweat, and her eyes, normally a bright brown, were deadened, as though she'd seen things Clara couldn't even dream of.

"Sam?" Clara repeated, grabbing at her friend's arm.

Sam blinked at her once and drew a shuddering breath. "I want to go home."

THE MONSTER AND
THE MOORS

DALE KNELT IN THE SOFT GROUND TO EXAMINE THE ANIMAL'S footprints. They were nothing like he'd ever seen before. They seemed cloven, like a sheep's, but elongated, like a human's, and tipped with small holes from its claws. The imprints were deep in the earth—slightly deeper than even Dale's, implying the beast was at least as heavy as a man.

"And the prints have been the same every time?" Dale asked.

The gaunt, haggard farmer who stood a few paces back gave a slow nod. "Aye."

Dale rose and rubbed his hands on his breeches. The farmstead was a twenty-minute walk behind them. To his left was the flock of sheep, protected in their gated field. To his right were the remains he'd been invited to see.

A ewe, horrifically mangled to the point of being barely recognizable, lay spread on the dewy grass. It had been partially skinned, and its limbs were torn from the body. Even Dale, who had seen his fair share of dead animals as a cryptozoology researcher, felt queasy.

"And this is the third time, correct?"

"Aye," the farmer replied.

Reports of a strange creature plaguing the small town of Wilton had been filtering through Dale's professional circle for several months. It wasn't until a farmer claimed to have seen the creature—described as taller than a human, with a skull-like face and viciously sharp claws—that Dale's interest had been piqued. Most of the cases he investigated turned out to be faked. But a sighting of a creature, even at night and from a distance, took effort to produce. Either the Wilton Monster was a very elaborate ruse...or he had a hot lead.

"I'm going to have a look around," Dale said, gazing about the countryside. "Thanks for your help."

"Aye." The farmer turned toward his farmstead and whistled for his dog to follow.

Dale set off toward the woods bordering the edge of the field. All of the reported attacks had happened at farms that bordered the same forest, which indicated that the creature lived within. The sun was falling low in the sky. Dale knew he couldn't stay out long without substantial risk, but his rifle was a comforting weight across his back, and he didn't intend to go far before returning to the village's inn.

The innkeeper had shared a plethora of stories about the monster and given suggestions about where to search for it. Dale suspected the keeper's stories became more and more embellished with every retelling, but he'd listened patiently, knowing he might pick up on a vital clue. Out of the dead animals—there were either nine or twelve; no one could agree on the number—most had been sheep, though there had also been two pigs and one chicken. In every case, the strange cloven animal prints had been discovered in the area.

Even if he didn't find anything noteworthy or even if it turned out to be a sham, it would make an excellent article to write up for his society's journal, and the story might even gain him some new sponsors.

The woods were thin and filled with sickly trees and sparse bushes. Dale walked carefully, aware that it would be all too easy to slip and fall into a pit or to twist his ankle. He kept his eyes focused on the ground, searching for any animal prints or signs that a hulking beast had been through the forest.

As he moved deeper into the trees, the light began to fade. Walking through the woods during the day was one matter, but he didn't fancy becoming lost in the dark and spending the night outdoors. He'd almost resolved to turn around when he caught sight of a shape in the distance.

Dale froze as the hairs across the back of his neck rose. He thought he'd seen a face between the spindly trees. Not a human countenance, though—but some sort of animal face, so white that it almost looked like a skull. Dale took a careful half step forward and caught a fresh glimpse of the creature between the trees. It stood on two legs but towered a full foot above him. It stood perfectly still, looking away, apparently captivated by something out of Dale's eyesight. Very carefully, barely breathing,

Dale pulled his rifle off his shoulder and raised the barrel to point at the creature's head.

Then a blinding pain burst across the back of his head. Bright lights flashed over his vision, and Dale fell to the ground.

When he opened his eyes again, he found himself on his back, staring up at the treetops. A noise came from not far away; it seemed to be a scraping, metallic sound. Dale tried to turn his head to look at it, but the pain coursed through his skull again, and an involuntary groan escaped him.

"Oh, awake, are you?" a familiar voice asked. The innkeeper's face swam into view. "That was fast. Well, Mr. Harrington. What do you think of my ruse?"

"Ruse?" Dale mumbled. The innkeeper nodded to one side, and Dale caught a glimpse of the monster again. What had appeared to be alive from a distance was, at close quarters, very clearly a costume made from animal skins and some sort of animal skull.

"It's been an awfully good boon for the town," the innkeeper said. The scraping sound continued. Dale managed to turn his head a little farther and saw the innkeeper was sharpening a knife on a rock. "It's saved my little inn from closing, at least, and others are reporting increased business from the tourists, too." He placed the knife to one side and knelt beside Dale, who struggled to raise his hands to protect himself. "But imagine how much more attention we'll get when renowned paranormal researcher Dale Harrington succumbs to the beast. Thank you, Dale, for what you're going to do for us."

The rock came down before Dale could defend himself.

ANGEL OF MERCY

Beryl rubbed at the bridge of her nose. It had been a long day—long *and* grueling. The patient's file open in front of her was full of hastily scribbled notes left by doctors and other nurses. She'd read it twice but still couldn't understand how the patient had died.

"See you tomorrow, Beryl," Mel said as she passed the desk. She was wearing more makeup than normal.

Must have a late-night date with the fellow she's been seeing. He must be exceptionally patient to agree to an eleven-thirty date.

"Have fun." Beryl gave her coworker a smile then looked back at the folder. It made no sense; the patient had been diagnosed with cancer, and although it had likely been terminal, he'd only been in the early stages. He should have had at least six months, if not several years. And yet, he'd died in the middle of the night, from unknown causes. The coroner's report had come back with an uncertain finding. No sign of a heart attack. No evidence of an overdose. No obvious injuries. He'd simply...died.

Beryl had been on shift on the night he'd died. He'd seemed well and alert. Then two hours later, she'd entered his room to give him his evening medicine, and he'd been gone.

She was reading through his notes to try to understand it. Her first thought was that he might have accidentally been given two lots of his blood pressure medication, but according to his notes, all medication had been administered in the correct quantities and at the correct time. *Unless he had an allergy we didn't know about...*

Beryl sighed and closed the file. She had the graveyard shift, and on a good night, there was very little to do once the patients went to sleep. The only staff left were Beryl, Dr. Stallen, Nurse Marlene, and Nurse Rochester. The ward felt virtually empty, save for the faint sound of footsteps echoing from deeper in the white polished hallways.

An idea was building in the back of Beryl's mind, but she hated to consider it. *Angel of mercy.* They were uncommon, but Beryl had read enough true crime stories to fear the concept of a doctor or nurse who deliberately extinguished their patients' lives.

You're letting your imagination run away with you. Beryl returned the deceased patient's folder to the filing cabinet. *You know everyone who was on last night, and they're all decent, hard-working individuals. No power plays. No overblown egos.*

And yet... Beryl hesitated, her fingers resting on the cold metal drawers. She glanced behind herself. The hallway was empty. Stark white lights reflected off the tiled floor and the multitude of posters stuck to the aging plaster walls. She rose and left the nurse's station.

Dr. Stallen and Nurse Rochester's voices came from the kitchenette, where they seemed to be in a debate about soccer teams. They would cope fine without her for a few minutes. Beryl crossed to the elevators and pressed the button to go down.

Old patient records were kept in the basement, and right next door to it was the morgue. Beryl tried not to think about the dead patients who would still be there, locked in the chilled, oversized drawers.

The number at the top of the elevator changed from 2 to 1, then 0, and finally B. The doors slid open, and Beryl stepped into the cold concrete hallway. It stretched on forever. She hurried through it, her footsteps echoing horribly in her ears, and tried not to look at the morgue's doors as she turned left into records storage.

She began opening drawers and working back through the folders, running her finger across the fading labels and colored stickers in search of familiar names.

Jane Edgell. She'd passed away from cancer a year before. Beryl pulled the folder out and flipped through it. She didn't like what she saw. Jane had been in decline for months, but was expected to live for another half year at least, with a chance of recovery after chemo. She'd been admitted to the hospital for a persistent cough and had passed away during the night.

Beryl let her breath out between her teeth and moved to the next folder. The hairs were rising on the back of her neck, and though she told herself she was overreacting and building up monsters in her mind, she came across yet another case of a patient who had mysteriously passed before their time.

After this sixth case, Beryl's fingers were shaking. *An angel of mercy…in our hospital. Who is it? They're clearly working frequently to have access to all of these patients over the last five years. That means I must have worked beside them dozens—or hundreds—of times. I've said hello when we've passed in the hallway. I've shared coffee with them, joked with them possibly, maybe even eaten with them. Worse, I've said good night to them, not realizing that they were planning to kill my patients once I was gone.*

A feeling of hopeless horror and guilt crawled across Beryl's back. She left the records room at a brisk walk, again averting her eyes from the doors leading to the morgue.

The angel of mercy, from what she could tell, only killed patients who were either nearing the end of their lives, were terminal, or had low chances of recovery. She tried to remember if any patients in her ward fit that description. The most likely target was Jerry Hoffenbacker, whose cancer had recently metastasized to his lungs. A combination of surgery and chemo might prolong his life, but for no more than a few years.

Beryl slammed her fist into the elevator's button. She'd left her three coworkers upstairs. If one of them were the angel…if the other two had been distracted, and Beryl had been busy in the basement…

Her breathing was shallow as she watched the elevator's numbers climb, praying she wouldn't be too late.

I knew this would happen eventually. Amber brushed a strand of loose hair out of her face and inhaled as the elevator doors opened. She turned toward the patient rooms. *Beryl isn't stupid. Of course she would figure out something was wrong. I just wasn't expecting it to be this soon.*

Dr. Stallen and Rochester were still talking by the kitchenette. That was good. They didn't look as though they would be moving any time soon. She turned right, toward Room 8, where Jerry Hoffenbacker was snoring.

I'll be safe for a while yet. Amber pulled a needle out of her pocket and discarded its plastic packaging. *Beryl won't suspect herself. Why should she? I've left no clues to tip her off, no signs that could make her suspect she has multiple personality disorder. As far as she knows, she's completely innocent.*

Amber pressed the tip of the needle into Jerry's neck, into the main artery, and injected a bubble of air. It would be a quick, painless death; the bubble would block a valve and force cardiac arrest without leaving signs of damage. Nothing would come up on the pathology tests. His death would be mysterious but not especially unusual. He was in the later stages of his life, after all.

Amber dropped the used needle into the sharps bin and returned to the elevator. She would ride it back to the basement level, then back up. By the time the doors opened a second time, Beryl would be back in control and ready to discover the newest death on her ward.

TUNE

Dan woke with a song looping through his mind. Its tune, low and slow, seemed familiar. He lay on his back for a few moments, listening to the notes and trying to place where he'd heard it before. It felt connected to his childhood. *Is it from a kids' TV show, maybe?*

He glanced to his left. His girlfriend, Jenny, was still asleep. He moved to wake her then remembered that it was a Saturday and she could sleep in. Dan sighed and rolled out of the bed, slipped his shoes on, and shuffled to the bathroom.

As he brushed his teeth, he found himself tapping his left hand on the sink in time with the song's beats. It was bothering him that he couldn't place it. It had a very specific tune, and he knew it meant something...or was used for something...or started something. *But what?*

By the time Jenny came out of the bedroom, Dan was already

nearing the end of his second bowl of cereal. She bent low over the table to see his face and gave him a warm smile. "What's buzzing around your bonnet this morning?"

"Hmm?"

"You look really preoccupied with something. And I know cereal nutritional information can't hold your attention that thoroughly."

Dan laughed and replaced the cereal box on the table. "Sorry, I've just got a song in my head. I'm trying to figure out where it's come from."

"Sing some for me. I might recognize it."

Dan had never been at all musically inclined. He couldn't remember words, hold a tune, or recognize major keys from minor. The song in his head was so intricate and unique that he was certain he wouldn't be able to express it, but as he hummed the notes, he felt great surprise and pleasure as it perfectly matched what was in his head.

"Don't sing any more," Jenny said after a moment. Her expression had changed to one of wary distaste. "It's an awful song."

Dan cut the tune short, feeling a surge of frustration. It felt somehow disrespectful and wrong to not complete the tune, like only singing half of the national anthem.

"Why? Do you know what it is?"

"No," Jenny said, sitting opposite him and pouring herself a bowl of cereal. Her face was still scrunched up, as though she'd smelled something bad. "It's just…really depressing. Like a funeral dirge, but worse."

"I think I remember it from when I was a kid. Like from a children's TV show or something."

Jenny laughed at that, though the sound wasn't as warm as Dan normally found it. "Wow, it would have to be a pretty rotten kids' show to include something like that. C'mon, let's not talk about it anymore. What've you got planned for today?"

"I promised Mum I'd visit her to change a busted light bulb." Dan drained the last dregs from his bowl to avoid speaking again. The song was still cycling through his mind, and he felt certain that if he could just focus on it for long enough, he would remember where he knew it from.

After Jenny had finished her breakfast, Dan kissed her goodbye and headed for the car. He only lived five minutes away from his mother, which he was grateful for; she was getting older, and little things—like replacing light bulbs and mowing the lawn—were becoming increasingly difficult for her. As he drove, he turned on the radio. He recognized the song that came on as a country ballad that he'd always enjoyed before, but on that day, it seemed impossibly shallow, and too preppy to tolerate. He turned off the radio and let the tune in his head wash over him again. *That's a real song,* he found himself thinking as the notes looped endlessly through his mind. *It's got depth and heart and meaning.*

By the time he'd reached his mother's house, he was humming the song again and enjoying the way he could reproduce the chords perfectly.

Dan's mother greeted him with a hug and a warm kiss. He wasn't sure if he was still growing or if she was shrinking, but she seemed to be getting smaller with each visit. She led him into the kitchen, where the bulb above the sink had blown the night before.

"This'll be fixed in a jiffy," Dan said, drawing a chair under the light while his mother put the kettle on. Even though the task would only take him a moment, Dan knew he wasn't likely to leave the house for a solid hour or two. His mother always loved company, and he could spend an entire afternoon talking to her about trivial matters and gossiping while they ate biscuits and drank tea.

As he unscrewed the light bulb, Dan began humming the tune again. The kettle finished boiling, but his mother didn't pour the water into the cups. He finished screwing the light in then hopped down from his chair to test the switch. The light came on without a problem, and Dan turned to his mother with a huge smile. "How about that?"

He realized something was wrong as soon as he caught a glimpse of his mother's face. Blood had drained from her skin, and her eyes were wide and tear-filled. Dan rushed to her and tried to help her into a seat.

"Are you okay? What happened? Do you feel dizzy?"

"You're singing that song again," was all she said. She let Dan ease her into the kitchen chair, and he hurried to make her a cup of tea. She seemed to be gathering her thoughts, and when Dan drew a chair up next to her, she took a deep, and seemingly resolved, breath. "Do you know what you were humming?"

"No. I woke up with it in my head this morning. I kind of remember it from when I was a kid, but I can't recall what it is."

"It's an old Scandinavian mourning song." His mother traced patterns on the table's wood with her index finger and seemed to be picking her words carefully. "It's not really ever sung anymore, even in Scandinavia. I didn't recognize it; your great-aunt did… she grew up in Scandinavia, you remember? She heard you the second time you began humming it, and told me what it was."

"Second time?"

"Yes, you've only sung it twice. Once when you were five and again when you were eight." His mother raised her eyes, which flickered uncertainly over his face. "The first time was the morning your grandfather passed away. The second was the day before your father died."

Dan stared at his mother, unsure of what to say, unsure of what *could* be said, as the song looped through his head relentlessly.

ROOM FOR RENT

THE SUN WAS CLOSE TO THE HORIZON WHEN HENRIK slowed his car outside the stone cottage. The unassuming two-story building, with its garden of hardy shrubs and winter-dormant rose bushes, blended into the village's old-world charm. Not for the first time that day, he wondered if the buildings had been deliberately designed that way to lure tourists.

The BOARD AVAILABLE sign in the window had caught Henrik's attention. He'd planned his trip across the country expecting to spend the night in the remote village and had been surprised to find it didn't seem to have any sort of hotel or motel. The nearest town was four hours away, and he was eager to get some food and sleep.

Henrik parked off the side of the narrow dirt road. Unless there was a shed or garage in the back, the cottage's owner didn't seem to have a car, just two bikes propped against the shadowed porch. Henrik cast a final glance back at the town, its gold lights glittering across the hill, then began climbing the steps.

"What'cha doing here?" a voice asked, and Henrik jumped. He hadn't seen the boy sitting in the old wooden chair at the back corner of the porch, and an embarrassed flush crept over his face.

"Uhh… I need a place to stay the night."

The boy's dark eyes darted over Henrik's face as a cold smile drew his lips apart. "Oh, really?"

Henrik hesitated, suddenly feeling uncomfortable. He was spared answering when the cottage's door swung open and a heavy-set woman with a wide reddish face leaned through the frame.

"What? Thom, are you scaring the guests off again?" she asked the boy.

He lurched out of his chair and skulked past the woman and into the house. It wasn't until Thom stood that Henrik realized he'd underestimated the boy's age; based on his height, he had to be at least in his midteens.

The woman turned to Henrik and gave him a sad, apologetic smile. "Sorry about him, love. He doesn't mean any harm. Were you looking for a place to stay tonight?"

Henrik hesitated for a second. *What's the alternative? Sleep in the car?* "Yes, please. How much?"

"Twenty for just the room," the woman said, glancing Henrik up and down as though to assess his worth. "Or thirty for dinner and breakfast included."

"I'll take that," Henrik said, fishing his wallet out of his pocket and sorting through the contents for thirty dollars. "It's been a long day. I'm Henrik, by the way."

"Barb." The woman took the money and ushered him inside with a wide smile. This time, Henrik hesitated for only a half second before crossing the threshold.

Henrik wasn't sure whether Barb was trying to apologize for her son's behavior or if it was normal for her to spend so much effort on their evening meals, but the dinner table was so laden with food that he could barely see the surly boy slouched opposite.

"Eat up," Barb urged Henrik, then turned to her son and added, "Don't fuss with your food like that. How'd you expect to grow up properly if you don't eat?"

The boy cast his mother an angry frown then settled his attention on their guest.

Henrik tried to focus on the food, which really was delicious, but the boy's eyes were darker than ink and felt almost hypnotic as they focused on him. It was the sort of stare he could have felt without even realizing he had company, and Henrik's skin developed goose bumps in response. He and Barb managed a smattering of small talk, which was more for politeness's sake than enjoyment. Henrik explained that he was traveling through the country to visit family, and Barb told him how her parents and grandparents had lived in their house for generations. All the while, the child—*teen,* Henrik reminded himself—scraped his fork across his plate without eating any of the food.

"We don't get so many tourists through here," Barb said, trying to push an extra serving of green beans onto Henrik's plate, despite his objections, "but it's always nice when we do. We're in no position to turn down the money. Are we, Thom?"

Thom, unblinking, opened his mouth and exhaled a breathy chuckle. Henrik frowned at him. *He couldn't possibly be suffering from a mental condition, could he? Insanity…at such a young age?*

Barb didn't seem happy at her son's response, and she scowled at his plate. "Eat. Why are you always so picky about your food? You'll grow up looking like a skeleton."

Again, the boy's mouth opened, and this time, his laughter, harsh, furious, and mournful all at once, rang in Henrik's ears.

"Enough," Barb said, dropping her cutlery beside her plate and pulling her son out of his chair. "If you can't behave when we have company over, you can eat in your room."

The boy's face turned murderous, and for a second, Henrik was afraid he was about to hit his mother. But then he turned, slouched through the doorway, and disappeared into the shadowed room beyond.

Very clearly embarrassed, Barb sighed and brushed a strand of hair out of her round face. "I'm so sorry."

Henrik waved away her apology as casually as he could. Raising a child with mental issues in the middle of the countryside seemed an insurmountable task. The town didn't appear to even have a proper hospital—just a single doctor's office he'd passed near the town's outskirts.

Barb gave him a tight smile. "Well, if you've had enough, shall I show you to your room?"

Upstairs was dark to the point of being dingy. Henrik placed his suitcase on the end of the narrow, quilt-covered bed and began sorting through it for his nightclothes. The lamps set into the walls were in desperate need of cleaning, and they sent heavy shadows about the room. There was at least three months' worth of dust on every surface.

Barb tapped on the doorway to announce her presence then entered, carrying a bundle of quilts. "In case you get cold tonight," she said, settling them beside Henrik's luggage. She hesitated then added, "Just so you know, I've locked Thom in his room for tonight."

"Oh?" Henrik glanced up from the luggage to see Barb was facing the bedroom window. She had a sad drawn look about her eyes, and he turned away, not wanting to embarrass her.

"Yes. He has...*problems* with people staying here. It's my fault. We need the money, so I don't turn anyone away. But he hates it now that he understands it. I forgot to lock his door one night, and he saw me carrying the body out back to bury it. He's never really been the same since."

The quilt dropped from Henrik's hand. "What—"

He didn't even have time to turn before the garrote slipped around his neck.

SNOW HUNTING

"Slow down," Ryan begged.

Max's boots dug up clumps of snow as he forced his way over the hill. He stopped at its crest and planted his fists on his hips to survey the valley in front of him. "Check this out! Hah, it's someone's holiday cabin."

Ryan tried to keep up, though he had forty kilos on Max and had become winded hours before. Despite the freezing temperatures, he was panting and sweating by the time he gained the hill's top. "Good for them."

"Wanna have a poke around?"

"What? Are you nuts?" Ryan stared at his friend, whose acne-scarred face had the manic grin he wore whenever he was about to get them into trouble.

"Why not? It's obviously a vacation house, and they're not going to be living in it off-season."

"I don't want to get…" Ryan trailed off, and Max laughed.

"Don't want to get arrested? Who by? The snow police? C'mon, ain't nobody crazy enough to be around here 'cept for us. Let's have a look in the rich guy's house. It'll give us a break from hunting."

Hunting had been Max's plan for that day. He'd taken his dad's gun and given Ryan a knife for the excursion. Ryan had been squeamish about the idea of gutting rabbits and deer, but after four hours of wildly off-the-mark shots and creating too much noise for them to have any hope of getting close to their prey, he was starting to think he might not actually need to use the blade.

"C'mon," Max said then took off down the other side of the hill in a windmill of waving limbs.

Ryan sighed and followed at a more sedate pace, being careful not to slip in the thick drifts. His friend was already at the cabin's door when Max reached the foot of the hill.

"He didn't even lock it!" Max yelled, shoving open the heavy wood door. "He's basically asking for people to look through his stuff. What a moron."

"Hey, slow down." Ryan staggered after his friend but hesitated on the house's threshold. The building looked expensive; he could imagine it belonging to one of the suited businessmen he sometimes saw picking up their children after school. He'd always envied those families; their kids had the best backpacks and shoes, showed off the latest games the day after their release, and talked about flying to France or Bali for their holidays.

That was, if he was honest with himself, the linchpin of his friendship with Max. They'd bonded over their hatred of "the rich brats," as they called them. Max was erratic, loud, and pushy, but Ryan had to admit, Max had made him see and do a lot of stuff he otherwise wouldn't have. Stealing. Skipping classes. Going hunting.

He sighed and entered the building. Max had dropped his backpack, gun, and gloves onto the wooden table that took up nearly half of the living room, and Ryan added his own backpack and knife to the pile. The room was large, richly furnished with furs and antlers, and surprisingly warm after the chill from the outside. He couldn't see his friend.

"Hey, Max?"

Max didn't reply for a moment, and when he did, his voice was strangely choked. "Get in here."

Ryan followed the voice down the corridor leading to the kitchen. A large freezer took up part of the room. Two marble counters and a collection of shelves covered the rest of the walls. It was clearly a hobby hunter's area to clean, prepare, and freeze the deer he'd shot.

Max stood in front of one of the counters. His face had paled. Ryan approached him carefully and slapped his shoulder. "What's up?"

"What does that look like to you?" Max asked.

Ryan's stomach flipped as he turned to the marble counter. It was coated in dried blood and some sort of long fur. "Uh…he's not good at cleaning up after himself, is he?"

Max carefully plucked one of the strands off the counter. He raised it to eye height. It would have been too thin to easily see except for the dried gore stuck to it. "Ever seen an animal with fur this long?" he asked.

Ryan hadn't. The strand was easily forty centimeters. "What're you saying?"

"This is hair." Max dropped the strand and stepped away from the counter.

Ryan opened his mouth to disagree, but no counterargument came to him. He raised his eyes from the bloodstained counter to look about the kitchen. It had all of the hallmarks of a hunter's home: multiple blades hung from hooks on the walls, boxes of plastic bags and wrap lay nestled in the corner, and a large bin sat in the corner. And, of course, there was the freezer.

"Don't open that!" Ryan said sharply, but Max ignored him. *Of course he won't listen to me. He never does.*

Max's face was blank as he raised the lid and stared at the box's contents. Ryan leaned forward, afraid of getting too close, but desperately curious to see inside.

At least two dozen plastic bags were arranged neatly in the deep freezer. Ryan saw a lot of flesh, but he couldn't even begin to guess what—or where—it had come from. He thought he saw pieces of skin that looked pink, though.

Max reached into the box and picked up one of the bags. He dropped it immediately, but not before Ryan saw the woman's features inside. Her lips were tinged blue from the cold, her eyes frozen open in an expression of shock, her long hair painted red by the blood that had run from her severed neck.

Ryan swore under his breath and grabbed Max's arm. "We've gotta get out of here."

For once, they were in perfect agreement. They scrambled down the hallway and back into the living room, where their equipment still waited for them on the table.

Max froze partway across the room. Once again, he was struck by how much warmer the cabin was compared to the icy landscape. *There's no way it should be this balmy. Not unless...*

He glanced toward the fireplace, where coals still glowed faintly in the grate. He tried to swallow, but his throat had tightened unbearably.

"Where's my gun?" Max said, anger rushing into his voice, but not quite capable of masking his fear. "What'd you do with it?"

"Nothing!" Ryan turned toward the table. Their backpacks and gloves were still scattered over the mahogany surface, but his knife was also missing. A piece of paper had been wedged under his backpack, though, and he pulled it free with shaking fingers.

I'm in the mood for some sport, the note read. *You have a two-minute head start. Run.*

WITCH'S BOOK

Avery's feet pounded across the hard, compact dirt as she raced after her twin sister. Their mother's words still rang in their ears: "You can explore, but stay close to the house and be back within an hour."

It was their first day at the Carillon farmstead. The moving truck had just left after depositing all of their earthly possessions. The teens had been cramped inside their car for nearly six hours, and both were itching to use their feet.

"Beat you!" Zoe crowed as she slammed her outstretched hands into the closest of the dark, twisted trees. Avery, breathless and flushed, staggered to a halt a few feet behind.

"It's not fair. You had a head start."

"Story of our lives." Zoe poked her tongue out then began dancing into the forest. It was a joke—Zoe had been born first, by barely twenty minutes, and liked to claim she was more mature. Avery had nicknamed her Granny in retaliation.

They wove into the forest, both admiring the towering trees that had likely been saplings when their great-grandmother had built the homestead. They'd never visited Carillon before—their mother had mentioned something about an old family feud— but, to everyone's surprise, the property had been bequeathed to them after Great-Grandmother Pearl's death.

A few feet into the woods brought them to a well-worn but narrow path. Zoe whistled as she saw it. "Look, it's still got her footprints in it."

"No, you're joking." Avery leaned close and saw, to her shock, there were indeed imprints of boots left in a section of dried mud. "But she's been dead nearly fifteen years."

"Maybe her ghost still walks this path," Zoe whispered into Avery's ear, forcing Avery to flinch away from the tickling breath.

"Cut it out."

"Scaredy cat."

Zoe laughed again and darted into the woods, disappearing among the trees. Avery had to jog to catch up. When she did, she found Zoe standing ahead of a small cottage-like shape.

"What is it?" she asked.

"Beats me." Zoe approached the door and tried turning the rusted handle. "Like a shed or something."

The handle squealed and broke off, and the twins glanced at each other guiltily.

"Don't tell Mum or Dad."

"Deal." Avery rubbed at her forearms, which were developing goose bumps since she'd stopped moving. "I don't like this place. Let's head back."

The door had been set at a slight angle and ground inward as gravity fought against rusted hinges. Inside was dim, but Avery could see a large stove, a wooden counter, and close to a hundred bunches of crumbling, long-dead herbs and leaves hung from a rack on the ceiling.

"Whoa." Zoe stepped inside and turned toward a shelf holding a collection of jars. "This is sick. Look, Ave—rabbits, lizards, and I don't even know what this one is."

The jars held a collection of preserved animals. When Zoe picked up one that contained a rabbit, the creature's fur swirled as it slowly rotated.

"This must've been Grandma Pearl's," Zoe muttered, replacing the jar and examining a series of dusty knives left out on the counter. "It's like…it's almost like…"

"I want to go home." Avery had her arms wrapped around her torso as she hesitated in the doorway. Her voice shook, and she licked her lips before repeating, "Let's go. Please."

Zoe turned a wide-eyed face toward her twin. "It's like she was a witch."

"Please! I want to go."

Zoe sighed, grimaced, and returned to the doorway. "Fine, all right. Stop being such a baby."

Their beds still hadn't been reconstructed, so Avery and Zoe slept on their mattresses on the floor. Even though this new house had twice the rooms as their old city apartment, they chose to continue sharing a bedroom.

Avery slept uneasily. Sometime after midnight, a dull light brought her back to awareness, and she rolled over to see Zoe had pulled her blankets up over her head and was reading a book by flashlight.

"What're you doing?" she mumbled.

"Shh." The blankets shifted as Zoe settled farther down. "I couldn't sleep. Just reading."

Avery scrunched up her face. The boxes containing their books were all downstairs, and she knew Zoe couldn't have walked over her without waking her. "What book?"

"None of your business."

"I'm serious. Tell me."

Zoe, looking irritable, flipped the blankets off her head and held up a narrow dark volume. "I found it in the cottage, okay? Now go to sleep."

"Zo! Are you crazy?" Avery sat up and scrubbed the sleep out of her eyes. "Put it away! What if it's cursed or something?"

"Jeez. I didn't want to tell you because I knew you'd flip out like this." Zoe rolled her eyes and shuffled around to face Avery. "It's not cursed. But listen to this. It's a book on spellcraft. Herbal potions, incantations, hexes, stuff like that. I think Grandma Pearl really was a witch."

Avery knew her voice was getting so loud that she risked

waking her parents, but she couldn't keep the urgency out of it. "Then you shouldn't be meddling with it."

"No, listen," Zoe insisted. A manic light had entered her eyes. "It says a witch can never truly be killed; her soul just passes into a new body. When a witch dies, her conscience and powers are transferred to the next-born child in the family." Zoe pointed to herself. "Grandma Pearl died just two months before we were born. I think… I think she might have passed her powers on to me."

"You *are* crazy!" Tears pricked at Avery's eyes. She snatched the book out of Zoe's hands and flung it across the room.

"It makes sense, though! Think about it—why did Grandma Pearl leave her house to our family? It's so that she could give her home and her witch's hut to her new body. I feel like if I can just study a bit, learn how it works—"

"Keep talking, and I'll scream," Avery threatened. "I'll scream and wake Mum and say you've been telling me horrible lies. She'll ground you for years."

Zoe's lips twisted. She carefully shifted back onto her haunches. "You're such a brat."

"You're not a witch. But you are freaking me out. I want you to leave that hut and all its junk alone," Avery spat, and rolled over before Zoe could argue any further.

When Avery stirred the following morning, Zoe's bed was empty. She bolted up herself and struggled into her shoes, already dreading where her sister might have gone and what she could be doing.

Her mother called something about breakfast as Avery ran downstairs, but she didn't even wait to respond. She tore across the clearing to reach the trees and found the narrow path.

She was breathless and had a stitch by the time she reached the hut. As she'd feared, the door stood open and a figure shifted in the dark interior. "Zoe?"

No response. Avery crept toward the cottage door, her skin prickling, and peeked inside.

Zoe sat at the table, multiple books open ahead of her, her eyes distant as she recited incantations to herself.

"Zoe!" Avery balled her hands into fists as she entered the cottage, and finally, her twin glanced up from the books. Her expression darkened.

"Get out of here. This is my stuff; I don't want you poking around."

"You're *not a witch*," Avery repeated, her voice rising to almost hysterical levels.

Zoe stood and loomed closer, her expression ferocious. She reached a hand forward and began reciting one of the phrases.

Avery's anger boiled over. She reached forward, snatched her twin's wrist in her hand, and channeled some of her power into it. Zoe yelped then screamed as invisible fire burned a ring around her hand. She pulled it back and cradled it against her chest, tears leaking from the corners of her eyes.

"You are not the witch." Avery summoned additional power

to rattle the jars on the walls and flutter the pages of the open books. "If you were, you would have had to work your whole life to keep your identity secret."

"But..." Zoe fell back against one of the bookcases, her face sheet-white. "But I'm the oldest..."

"No. Our parents mixed us up when we were babies." Avery stepped forward and sent a red thread of power out from her hand. Zoe tried to shy away, but it looped around her throat and tightened threateningly. "I'm not going to kill you," Avery whispered, leaning close to her twin. "You've been a good sister so far. But this is your last warning... Don't ever come into my nest, touch my ingredients, or read my books again."

THE WOMAN IN
THE MORGUE

FRANK LEANED ON THE SURVEILLANCE ROOM'S DOORFRAME AND glanced over the dozen screens set up above the desk. "Hey, Lest, how's it going?"

Lester, chip packet in one hand, swiveled his chair to give Frank a wide grin. "If it isn't my favorite nurse. Get your butt in here and grab a drink."

With a final glance at the nurse's station down the hallway, Frank slipped into the room and relaxed into the spare seat. "Thanks," he said, taking the offered soda. "It's been crazy tonight."

"Oh yeah?"

"Yeah, three patients coded. Can you believe it? Things have quieted down now, thankfully." He let his eyes skip over the screens, which showed every floor of the hospital. Frank loved coming into the security rooms during his break or when the nurse's station went through a quiet patch; he found it soothing to watch the bustle of the hospital without having to be involved. "Anything interesting happen tonight?"

"Not much," Lester said. "Had a family that tried to get out of the wrong door. They spent at least five minutes pushing and pulling on the handle before a nurse took pity on them and showed them to the right exit. Oh, and check this lady out. I reckon she must be from the psych ward. I have no idea how she got down there, though."

Frank leaned forward to look at the indicated screen. "Isn't that the morgue?"

"Yeah, it absolutely is. She's not a doctor. I have no idea how she would have gotten in there."

The woman, dressed in slacks and a jersey, walked up and down the length of the room, pausing to look at the labels designating which body was stored in each unit. She had her back to the camera, so all Frank could see were her fluttering hands and long black hair.

"You going to do anything about that?" he asked, shooting a critical glare at his friend. "It's a restricted section."

"Relax." Lester shook the chip packet at Frank, who waved it away. "I've already sent Paulo to bring her out. He should be there any time now."

Even before he'd finished speaking, the morgue's door opened. Paulo, their lanky security guard, ambled inside. He stopped just inside the door, his back to the camera, and faced the woman. She showed no signs of acknowledging his presence. After a moment,

Paulo unclipped his walkie-talkie and spoke into it. Its partner, which rested on Lester's desk, crackled, but no noise came out.

Lester swore at the black box as he picked it up. "Piece of garbage is malfunctioning again. Hey, Paulo, I can't hear you."

Paulo turned to look at the security camera and spoke again, though the footage was too grainy for Lester to read his lips.

"You're not coming through, idiot," Lester said, but Paulo didn't seem to hear him, either. The security guard turned and left the morgue, locking the door after himself. The woman either didn't notice or didn't care. She continued to pace, her hands twitching by her sides as she read the labels.

"Why's he leaving her there?" Frank leaned forward to scowl at the cameras.

Lester huffed in frustration and threw his empty chip packet to one side. "Jeez, no idea. Maybe she really is psychotic, and Paulo needs one of the nurses to help subdue her."

"Dibs not me." Even though his tone was casual, Frank found himself unable to look away from the woman on the screen. There was something disturbing about the way she moved, pacing awkwardly with her hands fluttering about her face, as she glanced at each of the tags. She was searching for something...*or someone.*

Paulo entered the surveillance room, ducking to fit his tall self under the doorframe. "Where'd she go?" he asked Lester.

Lester blinked at him then frowned. "Nowhere, idiot. Why'd you leave her?"

"What? She wasn't there. Did she leave the morgue or something?"

Frank tuned out the argument as he stared at the screen. The woman had turned to look behind herself, and in that second of seeing her face, he recognized her.

He'd seen her only briefly an hour earlier, but he knew he would never forget that face, with its bulging eyes and froth bubbling over the blue lips as he and a team of two doctors and four other nurses tried, and failed, to save her life.

UNDEPARTED

MARK STARTED AWAKE AND STOOD, KNOCKING HIS CHAIR TO THE floor. His heart thundered from a sickening nightmare, but the details were already slipping away like water through his fingers.

He ran his hands through his hair, pushing it off his sweaty forehead, and looked about the kitchen. Late-afternoon, blood-red sunlight sifted through the curtained windows to cling to the rough wooden furniture. Papers were spread across the table in front of him, but Mark merely glanced at them before crossing to the sink to fill a glass with water.

The sunset bathed the fields and bushes behind his rural property with a dim, sickly light. He'd never liked sunsets and never considered them romantic. They boded ill; it was the day's painful, final struggle to live before the night overpowered and smothered it.

That summer had been difficult. Infrequent rains had left the land parched. Red-tinted dirt blew across the property in thin gusts, dragged along by the hot wind.

The one thing that had never suffered was the billabong nestled behind the house. Even as the water table dipped, the natural lake maintained its rich-blue tone and bright-green water plants. It was the only soothing color for as far as Mark could see.

The billabong had been disturbed, though. A strange woman stood waist-deep in it, brushing her fingers across the surface as water dripped from her dark hair and white gown.

Mark dropped his empty glass back on the counter and grabbed the handgun off where he hid it on top of the cupboard. Mark's property was a long way from town, and he didn't recognize the intruder.

Mark tucked the gun into the back of his jeans as he pushed through the house's swinging door. He let it slam closed behind himself. The crack was loud enough to carry across the flat, barren lawn and reach the pond. But if the woman heard it, she gave no indication. She continued to sway gently, almost as though the wind were moving her, as she swirled her fingers through the water.

"Hey," Mark yelled, stalking across the lawn. "Hey, you!"

The woman said nothing, and she didn't turn. As he drew closer, Mark realized she was humming a low, somber tune. It seemed familiar, but he couldn't remember where he knew it from.

The hypnotizing swaying was unsettling, but he couldn't just leave her in his pond. With a final glance back at his home, Mark pulled off his boots, took a deep breath, and waded into the lake.

The water felt unexpectedly cold as it swirled around his legs—far colder than it should have been during the height of summer. It was colder, even, than it felt in the middle of winter. Mark shuddered but moved deeper into the water, closer to the woman. She continued to sway, humming the tune that teased at the corners of his memory.

"Hey," Mark said, as shivers ran up his back. "Hey, what're you doing here?"

The woman rotated slowly to face him at last, and Mark choked back a cry of shock.

Her face was ashen white and sickly. Dark smudges circled her eyes, which stared sightlessly into the distance. The water plastered strands of her dark hair to her face and dripped down her sunken cheeks.

Mark finally recognized the tune. It was a funeral dirge.

He took a half step back. The corpse opened her pale lips to speak. Her voice was faint, barely a cracked whisper, but the words carried to him as clearly as if they'd been screamed. "Murderer."

"What?" Mark took another half step back and nearly slipped on a mossy rock. He staggered, splashing water around himself, and the woman swayed toward him. Her eyes were directed at him but focused somewhere far behind his head.

"Murderer," she repeated, and her voice had developed an angry, dangerous note. Mark stumbled farther back, but his foot became tangled in a water weed. He fell, and the icy billabong enveloped him in its cruel embrace. As he struggled to pull himself upright, two horribly cold, viciously hard hands fixed around his neck. The woman's eyes, maniacally wide and blood-shot, gloated at him.

She was forcing him deeper under the surface, intent on drowning him. Mark fumbled behind his back to where the pistol was tucked then pulled it free and aimed it at the woman's face.

He could hear the crack even beneath the water. The pressure on his throat finally slackened. Mark lurched upright, exhaled a lungful of water then gasped in fresh air. The low sun painted the water a violent red. Mark took two steps backward, staring at the woman's body as it rose through the water to float just below the billabong's surface.

Her face was awfully, terribly familiar. He couldn't believe he hadn't recognized it before. It was the same face he'd fallen in love with four years earlier. It had beamed at him from behind a long white veil. The face had smiled at him, sadly, anxiously, as they gazed at each other above a table littered with final notices and creditor's letters.

A strangled sob escaped Mark's throat, and he raised the gun, almost automatically, to point at his own head.

Mark started awake and stood, knocking his chair to the floor. His heart thundered from a sickening nightmare, but the details were already slipping away like water through his fingers…

DOLL

"Okay, this one next!" Carol's mother threw her a present wrapped in plain brown paper.

Carol caught it, turned it over, and felt along the string for a tag. There was none. "Who's it from?"

"Not sure, sweetie. There might be a card inside."

Carol's family had gathered around their small, cramped living room for her birthday. In addition to her parents' presents, Carol had received an odd assortment of gifts from friends and distant relatives, and she was opening the stack of gifts while her parents let their lunch digest.

Carol, sitting cross-legged on the floor in front of the fireplace, tore off the string and paper wrap. Inside was an equally plain brown cardboard box, and she used her father's scissors to slice through the masking tape.

Inside was the strangest gift she'd ever received. Carol stared at it, a mixture of confusion and revulsion smothering her happy buzz.

"What is it?" Carol's mother, her wine glass nearly empty, sat in the large couch with her head resting against her husband's shoulder.

Carol wasn't sure if she had the words to explain, so she mutely held out the box so that they could see. A doll lay inside. Paint had been chipped off its cheeks, and its once-blond curls were dirty and frizzed. Its blue smock was torn on one sleeve and muddied around its hem, and its tiny hands were balled into fists as though it were angry at the indignity it was suffering.

"Ick." Carol's mother recoiled and set aside her wine glass. "I'm sorry, honey. That wasn't a nice gift. Who sent it?"

She shrugged. "No name. No card."

"Probably your brother," Carol's father grumbled to her mother, who shot him a disapproving glare and shuffled back so that she was no longer snuggled against him.

"Barry's been clean for six months."

"So he says."

"Besides," she continued, as though she hadn't heard, "even on his worst day, he wouldn't send my daughter this."

"Maybe it was a prank from one of the kids at school," her father conceded. "That little Hannah brat or something."

As her mother and father argued, Carol found her attention drawn back to the doll. Its ice-blue eyes stared up, seeming to fix on her with an intelligent intention. Hannah, the so-called brat from school, yelled insults and pushed people into the dirt when she wanted to prank them; she was nowhere near smart enough to come up with such a nuanced idea as the doll. Carol swallowed and closed the box's flaps over the neglected doll.

"Give it here," her mother said. "I'll get rid of it for you. What else did you get?"

Carol obediently handed over the box and picked out a new, brightly wrapped gift, but her attention was only half-focused on the task. As she unwrapped tickets to the concert she'd been begging to go to, she found she didn't care about them as much as she would have thought.

Carol snorted her way out of sleep. The night was chilly and quiet, and her room was cloistered in shadows, thanks to a sliver moon. She rubbed sleep out of her eyes as she tried to remember the dream that had woken her.

Something knocking…knocking to be let in…

As if on cue, a quiet *tap, tap, tap* came at her bedroom door. Carol's whole body stiffened. The sound was gentle but insistent—a polite request that wouldn't stay passive for long if it wasn't answered. As she'd expected, the taps came again after a moment, louder and harsher. Carol ran a tongue over her dry lips and slid out of bed. Goose bumps popped up across her flesh as the night air touched it, and she found her heart galloping as she neared the door. She opened it and let her eyes drop toward the floor.

The hallway was pitch-dark. Only two small shapes were visible: faintly glowing ice-blue eyes that stared up at her.

Close the door, her mind begged. *Don't let it in.* Her fingers twitched on the handle, but she kept the door open. Locking the doll out wouldn't keep it away. Denying it entrance wouldn't remove it from her life.

She reached out, her skin crawling, and picked up the small stubbly limbed figure. It felt unnaturally heavy and warm in her hands, as though flesh were hiding under the plastic shell. She was seized by a desperate need to kill it, to remove it from the earth, and turned toward the bathroom.

The room's light was harsh, so she shut the door to keep it from disturbing her parents. The light made her squint as she blinked at her pale reflection in the mirror. She hadn't noticed before, but the doll's hair color was an almost perfect match of her own.

She plugged the sink and turned on the tap's cold water—the monstrosity didn't deserve heat for its final moments—and waited until the water had risen two-thirds up the basin before plunging the doll under.

She held it there for a moment, watching as its dead blue eyes stared up at her, then she choked. Something thick and cold was filling her lungs. Carol retched, bent over the sink, and vomited a mouthful of water. She tried to draw breath, but instead of air, liquid filled her lungs.

The doll continued to gaze from under the water, and between gasping, vomiting sobs, Carol thought she saw its lips curve into a slight smile.

She pulled it out of the water and threw it aside. It created a harsh, wet slapping noise as it hit the tile floor, and finally Carol was able to replace the icy water in her lungs with oxygen. At the same time, a stinging ache began across her arm and chest— almost as though she'd been thrown against the floor.

She sank into a crouch beside the sink. It took nearly ten minutes to fully clear her lungs and slow her heart. The doll watched her from across the room the entire time.

At last, when the shaking in her limbs had eased enough that she could stand, Carol went to the doll and carefully lifted it. The eyes had too much awareness in them, and Carol was suddenly struck by the impression that the toy was smarter than she was.

She crossed to the cabinet and retrieved the first-aid kit. Inside was a needle, and Carol took a second to brace herself before pressing the miniature weapon into the doll's arm, just below its shoulder.

It stabbed through the plastic as though the hard shell had suddenly become soft. At the same time, a sharp, cutting pain sliced into Carol's arm. She withdrew the needle, her whole body shaking, her mind in shock, and carefully placed the doll back onto the edge of the sink before finding a towel to press against her bleeding arm.

I can't throw it out. If I throw it out, it will be damaged—maybe destroyed—and what will that do to me?

Carol pressed her hands over her face to muffle her quick, harsh sobs.

It's going to be okay. Carol drew in deep breaths then picked up the doll with shaking hands. *I don't have to throw it away. I can lock it in a cupboard. Somewhere no one ever looks. It will be safe there. And, more importantly, it can't hurt me.*

"I just don't get it," Carol's father muttered. He was sipping his morning coffee and ostensibly talking to her mother, but Carol felt him sending glances toward her every few seconds.

Her mother kindly nudged a box of cereal in Carol's direction. "What your father means, sweetie, is we don't understand why it has to be *that* one. We could get you a nicer toy if you want."

"No." Carol sat at the dining table, her doll propped on the counter beside her. It was dressed in clean clothes and with its curls washed and brushed, though its blue eyes still held the frosty, strangely human glint.

Her father's mouth twisted. "I don't like the way it looks. Can't you leave it in your room while we have breakfast?"

Carol gave her parents a thin, miserable smile. "I can't. She doesn't like being alone."

LEFT BEHIND

VIVIAN STARTED AWAKE. A VERY FAINT LIGHT ON THE HORIZON was bleeding away the stars, which meant it would be at least an hour before her alarm went off.

She rolled over to see her husband, Alan, still asleep next to her. His hair needed a trim, and it fell into his face, making him look like a shaggy dog. Vivian brushed the hair away from his eyes, but he didn't stir.

Something had woken her, but she couldn't remember what. *Some sort of noise…like an alarm.*

Vivian pushed herself out of bed and wormed her toes into her slippers before they chilled in the cold night air. She pulled her dressing gown over her pajamas and slipped out of the bedroom.

She glanced into her twins' room as she passed. Kara slept in the left bed, her wall covered in boy band posters and her bedside table scattered with makeup. Tara, on the right, was surrounded by pictures of horses and veterinary paraphernalia. Sometimes Vivian wondered how much easier Christmas shopping would have been if their interests aligned even slightly.

She moved downstairs to where the grandfather at the back of the hallway ticked quietly. As she entered the kitchen, she caught a glimpse of her neighbor, Mr. Richards, standing on his lawn.

Wearing only his socks and underwear, he was looking down the street at something beyond Vivian's view. She watched him for a moment then filled and turned on the kettle. If it had been anyone else, she would have called to him or gone out to check that he was okay. But Mr. Richards had yelled at her daughters while they were playing in the street the previous month, and Vivian still hadn't fully forgiven him.

As she waited for the kettle to boil, Vivian fished a bag of coffee out of the cabinet below the sink. She normally liked to grind the beans fresh, but the grinder was too noisy to use while her family was still asleep, and Alan became grumpy if he was woken too early.

The kettle reached its boil, and Vivian went to it. As she passed the kitchen window, she couldn't stop herself from glancing outside to see if Mr. Richards was still there.

He was, and so was the older woman from across the street, Evie, along with the teenage grandson who was staying with her.

Vivian stopped short, one hand on the kettle, as she frowned at them. They weren't talking. They weren't even standing close to each other. But they were facing the same direction, and their chins were tilted upward as though they could see something in the sky—something that they found too captivating to look away from. *Is there a lunar event this morning? A comet, maybe?*

They weren't moving, and Vivian had no desire to go outside, so she turned to the back of the house and went into the laundry room. She emptied the previous night's washing into a basket and refilled the machine, though she didn't turn it on. She left the basket beside the back door for when it was light enough to hang it and returned to the front of the house. This time, her curiosity was too strong to be denied, and she went to the window.

Half the neighborhood seemed to be out of their houses. She recognized many of them, though a few were unfamiliar. They all faced the sky with slack jaws and intent eyes.

Vivian crossed her arms over her chest. Suddenly, it didn't seem so important to let Alan have his extra hour of sleep. She ran up the stairs, no longer trying to keep her footfalls quiet, and pushed into her bedroom. The bed's blankets had been cast back, and the room was empty.

"Alan?"

Vivian moved to the bathroom, but her husband wasn't there. She turned and saw his slippers were still tucked neatly under the bed.

Rising panic threatened to choke Vivian as she ran to her twins' room. She wrenched open the door and bit back a choked cry. Two identical beds sat empty. Two very different pairs of shoes lay on the ground, both waiting for their owners to wake up. The twins were gone.

Back down the stairs, Vivian called for Alan, then Kara and Tara, in a final, desperate bid to find them still safely inside. When they didn't answer, she tightened the dressing gown around her torso and pushed through the front door.

The street was packed. Everyone in her neighborhood seemed to have gathered on the road at five thirty in the morning, all to stare at the sky.

Vivian looked up. She couldn't stop herself. She had to know what had captivated them and compelled them to stand in their underwear and dressing gowns in the freezing cold morning.

The sky, still dark and spotted with stars, seemed exactly the same as always. Vivian searched for any kind of aberration or change without success, then she turned back to the crowd.

She found Alan easily. He was tall and stood nearly a head above his neighbors. She couldn't see Kara and Tara, though; they weren't with their father, and the gathering had become too dense to find them easily.

Vivian pushed through the crowd to her husband and shook his arm. "Alan? What's happening? What are you doing out here?"

He didn't move his eyes from the sky. He didn't even blink. But his mouth opened, and he said, in a voice that was very much unlike his usually cheerful tones, "It's time. Get ready."

"Alan?" Vivian shook him more frantically, but she couldn't break his attention. To her shame, she found herself crying, and she rubbed her sleeve over her damp cheeks as she ran through the crowd.

Back inside her home, Vivian grabbed the kitchen phone off

its hook and dialed the emergency help line. She shifted from foot to foot as the phone rang—and rang and rang and rang.

"Come on," Vivian muttered, gripping the phone tightly in her sweating palms. "Come on, answer!"

The incessant ringing noise mocked her. Vivian couldn't stop herself from picturing the police station, its rooms emptied of officers as they filed outside to stare at the sky. She dropped the phone and ran back to her home's front door, intent on finding her daughters and dragging them back inside, if nothing else.

The street was empty.

Vivian clapped a hand over her mouth. She stepped onto her front porch and stared up and down the length of the road, where barely moments before, hundreds of souls had gathered. The sun had just barely breached the hill on the horizon, and its golden light spread across the road. Vivian rotated on the spot, staring at the empty street and the empty houses as she found herself facing the idea of being the last person left on earth.

UNDERHOUSE

XAVIER BIT THE FLASHLIGHT BETWEEN HIS TEETH AS HE PULLED the gloves on.

His mother stood nearby, hands clasped, looking anxious. "I'm just worried you'll get stuck."

He dropped the flashlight into his hand and laughed. "Gee, relax. I haven't gotten *that* fat."

"You were a kid last time you went down there…"

"There's plenty of room." He pecked her cheek then bent down by the door that led into the crawlspace below their home. "You worry too much."

Before she could argue any more, he lurched forward, through the small doorway, and into the cool, dry air of the section below their house.

Despite his jovial reassurances, the space did feel a lot tighter compared to when he'd made the trip when he was ten. Back then, there'd been room to crawl; now his chest was too deep to allow him anything except scrabbling forward on his belly.

The wooden beams were filled with cobwebs, long abandoned by spiders who had either starved or moved on to greener pastures. The ground was a heavy layer of dust that plumed up every time Xavier shifted. He wriggled far enough into the hole that he could no longer hear his mother's nervous breathing, then he turned on the flashlight.

He'd lived in their small, rural property his entire life, but it was still disconcerting to try to remember the house's layout without the familiar walls and furniture to guide him. He closed his eyes and tried to visualize the route to the workroom, where a new wire needed to be threaded under a wall. The workroom was near the left side of the house, so he turned that way, creeping across the dust and breathing through his nose to keep his tongue clean.

Xavier judged he was somewhere near the back of the lounge room when a large, lumpy shape by the wall drew his notice. It was a backpack, so long neglected that it had accumulated its own layer of dust. Xavier shimmied closer. He recognized the black fabric and red dragon design emblazoned down one side. Memories brought a smile to his face. He was tempted to open it, to search through the familiar contents, but reluctantly, he turned away. He had a job to do first.

In the distance, a small sliver of light marked his destination. A matt of black cables looped down from between the wooden beams, then back up to disappear into the floor several feet away. Xavier wriggled to them then tapped on the wood.

"You all right, love?" his mother called from the room above. He didn't want to open his mouth and let the dust inside, but he knew she would panic if she didn't get an answer.

"Fine."

"Okay, here we go, love." A wire appeared in the slice of light around the existing cables. Xavier rolled onto his side to grab it, then pulled it down and wriggled to where it needed to be returned to the house, one room over. His mother hurried out of the workroom and into the bedroom, her footsteps shaking down tiny streams of dust to mark where she walked. Xavier waited until she was in position before threading the wire through the hole.

"Got it!" she cried, and the cable was tugged from his hands. "Come back out now, love, and you can wash off all that grime."

That sounded like a damn good idea to Xavier. It took him a moment to maneuver into the right position, then he began dragging himself back toward the exit.

A lumpy shape, not unlike the discarded backpack, lingered near a support pillar to his left. Xavier had initially intended not to look, but his curiosity was too great, and he found himself turning toward it.

A boy, long dead, lay among the dust. The mouth lolled open, showing a withered, blackened tongue, but the eye holes were empty. Blood had run from the cut throat and stained the front of his T-shirt, which had blackened with age then been softened into gray by a coating of dust.

What was surprising, though, was that the body hadn't decayed.

Xavier had expected Chad to turn skeletal in the decade he'd been there. Instead, he had withered and dried—almost mummified. Xavier knew better than to touch it, but he suspected the skin would be firm and leathery if he did.

Thinking back to the summer he'd killed Chad, he remembered the days being almost unbearably hot. He supposed that was likely the cause; the air had been so dry, it had dehydrated the body rather than decayed it. That would explain why there hadn't been more odor. His mother had only remarked about it twice and never actually gone looking for a cause.

Seeing his bully's face again after so much time, Xavier felt neither triumph nor guilt. The husk was so far from human that he barely felt anything at all. Still, he allowed himself a very slight, very small smile as he continued toward the door leading back outside.

TOXIC

RITA GROANED AND PRESSED HER PALMS INTO HER TEMPLES. THE descriptions of melted skin, blinded eyes, and third-degree burns wouldn't ever leave her, she was sure.

It had seemed like a cushy job when she'd taken it: be the receptionist for a remote branch of Kamadero Manufacturing, one of the country's largest chemical processing plants. The building was only used for infrequent business meetings. Most days, Rita was lucky to see another human being. Coming from the service industry, she'd thought the desk job felt like a full-time holiday. It only took half an hour to reply to emails and phone messages each morning, and Rita liked to divide the rest of her time up between browsing social media, watching online videos, and playing whatever addictive game was hot that week.

At least, that had been her routine until that Monday, when she'd been given the task of compiling statistics for the company.

From what she understood, the job had been delegated multiple times before it had landed in her lap. Rita had no underlings to foist the task onto. She was stuck compiling spreadsheets from the medical reports of forty-eight individuals who'd been involved in a malfunction at one of the warehouses in Mexico. From what she'd gleaned, a distributor hadn't followed storage guidelines, and the results were horrific. The company was simultaneously trying to keep tabs on the victims and minimize its liability.

She was eternally grateful that no photos had been included in the files. The descriptions were bad enough. She created a new line on the spreadsheet, entered the patient's name, and began copying their report. Blistered burns over thirty-five percent of the body. Lost eyesight. Permanent scarring of the facial, neck, and arm tissue. The details were followed by a long list of measurements and severity markings.

Rita exhaled and leaned her neck back to stretch its muscles. Her desk faced the front door of the building, which was a long, hedge-lined driveway leading to the parking lot. An elderly woman, bent double by age and wearing a shawl over her head, shuffled along the drive toward the office. Rita sat up a little straighter. She'd been told the documents were confidential. She was pretty sure it was only a legal precaution, but she still scooped up the piles and hid them in the drawer at the bottom of her desk.

When Rita looked back at the glass doors, the woman was gone. Rita blinked at the empty pathway. There were no nearby buildings the woman could have gone to, no paths branching off from the driveway. She'd simply vanished.

The chair creaked as Rita rose out of it. She moved to the door and peered through, searching the path, the hedges, and the lawn surrounding it, but the area was empty.

Did I imagine it? Are the medical reports actually sending me crazy? Rita shook her head and turned away from the doors. The large room felt too quiet for comfort. She switched the radio on and exhaled as it started playing some eighties tunes. *I need a break.*

She went to the kitchen to make a cup of tea. The kettle's light blinked on, and it started to heat as Rita put a mug on the counter and fetched the milk from the fridge.

The microwave's front was faintly reflective, and Rita glanced in it as she passed. She saw her face, her hand holding the milk carton, and the wobbly shapes of the kitchen appliances. And, farther behind her, the cowled figure of an elderly woman hunched against the far wall. A sharp gasp froze in Rita's throat as she swung around and dropped the milk, but the room was empty.

Her hands shook, and her heart thumped painfully as she stared around herself, scrutinizing the room, then finally looked back at the microwave. She could still see her drawn, tense face in the mirrorlike surface, but the woman was gone.

Rita's feet were wet. She looked down to see the floor was coated with milk from the carton she'd dropped. She ran a trembling hand over her face and went to find a towel.

There's no way the woman could have gotten into the building, she told herself as she mopped at the milk. The front door desperately needed oiling and squealed whenever it was opened. She would have heard it, even over the boiling kettle and the radio...

The radio. It wasn't playing cheerful eighties tunes anymore. Instead, it made a clicking, screeching sound—exactly like a record that had gotten stuck in a scratch.

Rita kept still for a long time, hunched over the wet cloth. The sound didn't change, and the longer she listened, the more she thought she could hear slow, rattling breathing in the background. Without turning her back to the kitchen's entrance, she picked up the milk-soaked cloth, placed it in the sink, then quietly walked toward the reception area. "Hello?"

The room was empty, but the radio continued to play the same scratching noise. Rita stepped toward it slowly, feeling as though eyes were watching her. She stretched a trembling hand out and smacked the radio off. The infuriating record-scratch sound seemed to echo through her head as she turned and scanned the room.

This is ridiculous. Am I going crazy? Did someone get into the building without my knowing?

She still had the awful creeping feeling that she was being watched as she returned to the kitchen. The half-empty milk carton waited where she'd left it on the counter, damp and slightly dented from where it had been dropped. She wiped it clean and opened the fridge's door to replace it.

The fridge, compact and cheap, was scantly filled. Rita's lunch sat on the top shelf, and a few condiments and jars were lined up neatly on the third shelf. In between, nestled in the middle of the second shelf, was a dead sparrow.

She almost dropped the milk again. The bird was twisted around, and the feathers were burned from at least half of the body. She could see the thin, splitting skin below, caked with some sort of green, caustic-looking slime. The stench of chemicals reached her nose and made her gag as memories of the burn victim notes flashed through her head.

The urge to be sick rose, and Rita slammed the door. She thought she heard a breathy sigh behind her but was already running for the door.

The bird hadn't been there when she'd taken the milk out of the fridge. She shuddered and clutched at her face. Someone was in the building.

Her desk stood between her and the front door. A stab of shock hit her as she saw the files she'd hidden in the drawer were arranged neatly over the counter, lined up one after another. A red pen had been used to scrawl huge, angry words across the pages. *MURDER. GUILTY. MURDER. GUILTY.* The phrase repeated over and over, sometimes so large that the letters ran off the sides of the papers and stained the desk, sometimes so tiny that they fit between the margins.

Rita's head buzzed as she gawked at them. She skirted around the table, her back to the wall to give her as much space as possible. One of the pages fluttered, and she flinched, but she didn't dare avert her eyes. Her back bumped into the glass front door. She reached behind herself to twist the handle, but it was frozen. She turned. Two opaque eyes stared into hers.

The age-bowed woman on the other side of the glass pulled the lace shawl off her shoulders. Her hair was burned off, and her blistered face was caked with the green slime. Her dead eyes, bleached white, stared into Rita's.

Rita screamed. She covered her eyes and staggered backward, moving into waiting arms. Two ice-cold hands wrapped around her neck and squeezed, choking out her cry.

THE LAST BUS

RAJ GROUND HIS TEETH AS HE LEANED HIS FOREHEAD ON THE BUS timetable and tried to read the routes. The twenty-six, twenty-eight, and forty stopped there, but it didn't say which ones, if any, went to Calgary.

He glanced at the houses lining the street. He didn't like to think their occupants might be watching him, laughing at how obviously confused he was. The familiar tight feeling of humiliation built in his stomach, but he pushed it down.

You've got nothing to be ashamed of in this neighborhood. It's only two steps away from being a slum; probably half the people who live here are illiterate.

A squeal of tires disturbed Raj. He turned and saw, to his surprise, a bus had pulled up beside him. *I didn't even hear it coming.*

He tried to see a direction or a number on the bus's face, but it had neither. The doors opened with a quiet *whoosh*.

"Hey," Raj said, and the driver, a plump, middle-aged man with a pleasantly smiling face, leaned toward him. "Where're you heading?"

The man laughed. "All sorts of places, kid. Where d'you want to go?"

Raj glanced at the dilapidated houses around him. He hadn't expected anyone who managed this sort of route to be *pleasant*, let alone friendly. The driver looked like the sort of person who belonged in comfortable upper-middle-class suburbs, managing a private school's bus, perhaps.

"Uh…" Raj glanced back at the sign's map. He'd had the vague idea of going to Calgary, where one of his brother's friends lived, but he could be flexible. More than anything, he wanted to get out of the neighborhood. "You passing near Calgary at all?"

"Sure am," the driver said, beckoning Raj aboard. "We're looping through a few other suburbs first, though, so it's going to be a long trip. That okay?"

Raj hesitated, one foot in the bus. A long trip meant a lot of money, which he didn't have. "How much?"

The bus driver gave him an appraising look, his blue eyes scanning Raj's stained hoodie and torn jeans. "Kid, I hope I don't seem out of place saying this, but you look like you're in some sort of trouble."

If an alcoholic with a raging temper and peculiar ideas about what fatherhood meant counted as trouble, then Raj was in a whole lot of it. He felt his face heat as he gave a dismissive shrug.

"Hey," the driver said, and the warm smile grew over his face. "We all need a hand up sometimes. The ticket's on me."

Raj didn't know what to say. He mumbled some sort of thanks as he stepped onto the bus, then the doors drew closed behind him as Raj looked for a seat.

The bus held an eclectic collection of passengers. Near the front was a young, pretty woman with dyed-blue hair and nose piercings. Three rows behind her sat a businessman with a limp paper folded over his hands. A little farther back was a teenager a couple of years younger than Raj. Judging by his sickly pallor and the way he shot paranoid glances at his companions, Raj suspected he'd been dipping into some less-than-legal substances. A man who seemed to be homeless lounged against one of the windows, sleeping. Two middle-aged women sat at the other side of the bus, near the back, knitting. And a girl with smeared mascara stared out the window with studied silence.

Raj took a seat behind the pretty girl near the front and leaned back so he could rest his shoulder against the window. The girl shot him a bright smile as he passed. Raj smiled back, against his better judgment.

"All settled?" the driver called as he put the bus into gear.

Raj felt a shock pass through him. When they'd been talking, the driver had held his hands in his lap, where Raj couldn't see them. As he'd placed them back on the steering wheel, Raj was faced with the sight of ten long dark-yellow nails.

It was so bizarre and out of character for the otherwise bright and tidy driver that Raj couldn't take his eyes away. The nails were at least three inches long, and seemed sharpened at the tip.

"Bad day?" a husky voice asked. Raj startled and turned toward the pretty girl.

"Wha…?"

"You looked pretty deep in thought there," she said. Her voice was lower than Raj would have expected, and he found he quite liked it.

A hesitant smile started to grow across his face, but he squashed it quickly. "Well, not the best, but, uh…"

"Hey," a voice barked from farther back in the bus. "This isn't the way to Hyde Street."

Raj turned to see the drugged-out kid had spoken. He looked agitated, squirming in his seat and stealing glances at the two knitting women who sat opposite.

The bus driver glanced into his rearview mirror, a sunny smile lighting up his face. "You're right," he said simply then addressed the rest of the bus, "Think we've got enough?"

A chorus of voices answered.

"Yeah."

"Good for me."

"Let's do it."

The driver took a sharp turn and picked up speed, weaving the bus through some of the darker, lesser-used lanes. Raj felt unease tickle at his stomach. He glanced at the pretty woman, who had turned in her seat to face him. Her large dark eyes crinkled into a smile. She didn't seem concerned at all.

Raj turned to look at the rest of the bus. The knitting women and the businessman all looked unaffected. Only the druggie, the teenage girl with the smeared mascara, and the homeless man, who'd woken from his doze with a confused snort, seemed in any way disturbed.

"What's going on?" Raj asked, turning back to the driver. He didn't recognize the area they were in, but it looked industrial. Warehouses lined the road, and he couldn't see any other traffic.

"Just wait a moment," the driver said, "and you'll understand."

Raj didn't want to understand. He wanted to get off the damn bus with its damn creepy occupants and its damn strange driver with his damn long nails.

"What's wrong with your hands?" the druggie's voice rang out again, and Raj turned. The kid was glaring at the knitting women, who both gave him equally polite smiles. Raj leaned forward in his seat to see them more clearly, but both women had their knitted scarves draped over their hands.

Raj felt, all of a sudden, that the hidden fingers were a very bad sign. He found his eyes roving the rest of the bus's occupants, checking their hands. The druggie's, the homeless man's, the crying teenager's, and his own were all visible. But the knitting ladies had theirs covered with their yarn, the businessman had the newspaper draped over his, and the pretty woman in front of Raj had hers tucked into her pockets.

"What…" he began. Then the bus pulled to a stop.

There were no streetlights. No houses. No cars. Raj stood and prepared to bolt for the door, but the driver pressed a button, and the doors locked with a quiet click.

"Let's eat," the bus driver said simply. And suddenly, all of the hidden hands in the bus were exposed as the knitting and newspapers were put away.

Raj felt a scream build in the back of his throat, but he already knew no one would hear him. The creatures with long yellowed nails moved with deceptive speed. Both knitting women descended on the druggie, their jaws opening wider than a human's possibly could have as sharp, sharklike teeth extended forward. The motion was almost too fast for Raj to follow, but he caught the abortive, gurgled scream that cut off in a spray of blood. The suited man dropped his paper and leaped over the back of his seat to reach the half-asleep homeless man. The bus driver loped forward, past Raj, his eyes fixed on the terrified teenage girl. A fleck of blood hit Raj's cheek, and he turned, horrified, to find the pretty girl's dark eyes an inch from his face.

"Sorry." She was smiling, but her breath was contaminated with something sick and rotten as she extended her yellow claws toward Raj. "Today's about to get an awful lot worse."

HOUSE FOR SALE

SMILE, PAM COACHED HERSELF. SHE WAS WATCHING A YOUNG couple walk through the kitchen, noting the damage to the cabinets and the broken tiles that exposed the dirty plaster beneath. *Look attentive but not obsessive. And for the love of all that's merciful, don't let them see how much you hate this house.*

"Do you think the owner would be open to negotiation?" Paul, the husband, asked. He had huge eyebrows that had grayed before his hair. They reminded Pam of fuzzy caterpillars.

"I'm sure they would." Pam tried to inject just the right level of warmth into her voice. *They've got to think you're on their side. They've got to trust you.*

Paul was clearly trying not to let his interest show, but it slipped through in the way he rocked on the balls of his feet and kept glancing at his wife. Melissa, the young bride, clearly had the final say in the purchase, but she seemed interested, too.

This might be it, Pam thought, beckoning her companions into the living room to show off the dusty stone fireplace and scratched wooden floors. *After eight years on the market, I might actually sell the Hunt Street property.*

The house was notorious in real estate circles. No one had been able to get anything more than vague curiosity since it was listed for sale. During that time, the house had deteriorated. Stains crept down the plaster walls, and water damage peeled up the bases of the cupboards. That wasn't the main reason the house remained empty, though.

"It would make a great project for anyone interested in home improvements," Pam said, sneaking a glance at Paul. He seemed the sort of person who fancied himself a handyman, and his eyes lit up at the prospect.

"It's going to be a lot of work," Melissa said.

C'mon, Melissa, don't nuke this on me. I could really do with the commission.

"I've been looking for a hobby to take up on the weekends," Paul supplied, and Pam beamed at him.

Melissa didn't answer. The door at the back of the living room had caught her attention. "What's through there?"

"The basement," Pam said, stepping forward. "Would you like to see inside?"

Please say no. Please say no. Please say no...

"Sure," Melissa said, and it took a lot of effort for Pam to keep the smile on her face. "Absolutely."

She'd never been into the basement. She'd never had any desire to go into the basement. But if the newlyweds wanted to see it, who was she to say no?

"It hasn't been opened in a while," Pam said, searching through her key ring. The keys were all old, bronze, and partially rusted, though they had plastic tags to list which rooms they unlocked. "It might be a bit mildewy down there."

Melissa's hand fluttered to her belly, which had the barest hint of a bump.

Ahh, so it's going to be a family home, then. I'm not sure it's a place I'd want my kids growing up in, but if they want to take it off the market, I won't complain.

Pam had gone through her key ring without finding the basement tag, so she started sorting through it again, more carefully. "Sorry. I can't seem to find it—"

"That's fine." Melissa turned away from the door, to Pam's great relief. "Can we see upstairs, instead?"

"Absolutely." *Smile, smile, smile.*

They knew the house's history, Pam reminded herself as she climbed the stairs. The law said her real estate company couldn't sell the house without disclosing any facts that could dissuade a buyer. *And, boy, the Hunt Street property has enough facts to write an encyclopedia.*

The steps creaked under Pam's sneakers, and tiny sprinkles of dust fell from the ceiling. She tried not to touch the railing or the wall. The house had always felt dirty to her. She knew the crime scene cleaning team had been thorough, but even so, the building felt tainted in a way that no amount of bleach could cure.

Don't let them see it affecting you. Let them think it's a nice fixer-upper with a quirky history. If you can make this sale, you'll never have to think about the house again.

On the top floor, Pam led the couple through the bedrooms as quickly as she could without looking as though she were rushing them. "Here's the master bedroom." *That's where Mr. and Mrs. Bellet were murdered in their sleep by an unknown assailant. He used an ax, did you know? Apparently, the blood sprayed all up that wall there and dripped off the ceiling. The crime scene cleaners had to strip the room entirely and tear up most of the floorboards to purge it.*

"Through here is the children's bedroom." Pam gave Melissa an extra-bright smile and a knowing wink. *Little Frankie Bellet's blood ran through the mattress and stained the floor. Please don't Google search for the pictures. I did, and I'd give anything to forget them.*

"And the spare room." It was a pretty, airy area. The killer's message, scrawled in blood across the opposite wall had been scrubbed and painted over. Sometimes, when Pam glanced at the wall out of the corner of her eye, she imagined she could still see the words there. *"This house is mine."*

Four years of hunting, four years of failed or inconclusive DNA testing, and four years of the police chasing increasingly flimsy tip-offs had all been in vain. The killer had never been found. That chilled Pam the most. The crimes had been terrible, yes, but the potential that they could be echoed in another home, with another family… Still, it didn't seem to bother the newlyweds.

They were more interested in the dirt-cheap price and how large and well situated the building was. The atmosphere, which made Pam's skin crawl every time she crossed the threshold, didn't seem to touch them.

Pam pretended to gaze out of the window at the aged elm tree in the backyard while the couple talked in hushed tones behind her. Paul loved the house. His eyes were bright, and he was gesticulating erratically, apparently talking about the modifications they could make to turn it into their dream home.

What was more, he seemed to be winning Melissa over. The mother-to-be gave a small nod, and Pam sensed it was her cue to step forward.

"We'd like to make an offer to your owner," Melissa said.

Pam tried to keep her smile from becoming too wild. *Did I seriously do it? After eight years, am I finally getting the Hunt Street house off my list?*

"Absolutely," Pam said, ushering them out of the room and toward the stairs. She was desperate to get outside and away from the toxic aura saturating the building. "How about we go over the details in my office? I'll make you a lovely cup of tea while we work out your offer."

As they headed toward their cars—Paul and Melissa into a van that had clearly been bought with the intention of expanding their family, and Pam into her Mini that let her park in even the most choked city streets—Pam stole a final look at the Hunt Street property. Its gloomy façade stared back. *No, it's more than gloomy. It's menacing. Even the windows, from the high attic arches to the little square that belongs to the basement, look grim.*

The basement window—!

Pam did a double take, but the window was empty. She felt her mouth open a fraction as her heart rate shot up and sweat slicked her palms. *I didn't imagine that, did I...?*

"Ready?" Paul asked, and Pam knew for certain her smile was shaky.

You're so close, Pam. Don't lose the sale.

"Of course," she said, sliding into the front seat of her car, trying to erase the image of the sallow, furious face watching them through the basement window.

DIAGEN

PASCOE SAT NEAR THE BACK OF THEIR SMALL CANOE, ONE HAND braced on the side of the boat and the other holding the motion picture camera as steady as he could. Behind him, Guide used a long pole to slide their canoe through the marshy water systems.

It wouldn't be clear in the black-and-white film, but the surrounding landscape was a thousand shades of green. Gray-green lichen hung like giant curtains of lace from the towering moss-coated trees. Clouds of tiny shimmering insects hovered above the water's surface, setting up a constant drone that steadily worked itself into Pascoe's brain.

"A little to the left," he instructed Guide, pointing in the direction he wanted to ensure the message got through.

Guide spoke just enough English to be hireable, but no more. Communication was so difficult that Pascoe still hadn't figured out his ward's name. The short, perpetually smiling man responded to the title "guide," though, so that was what Pascoe called him.

Guide obediently turned the boat, and Pascoe let the camera pan across the landscape. Details like the scum floating on the water's surface and the birdcalls wouldn't come across in the theatrical release. Even so, the landscape was dramatic enough to earn him a good sum for the footage, even if he never found the Diagen.

Rumor had it that a giant water creature resembling a croco- dile lived in the swamps of Venezuela. The legends contradicted each other more often than they concurred, but all agreed the ancient beast was more than twice as long as a man and had rows upon rows of vicious teeth.

When he'd started the expedition, Pascoe had been thrilled to discover that Guide claimed to have knowledge of the Diagen. Of course, after hiking across the country for three days, Pascoe had realized Guide would have sworn he was capable of flying to the moon if he thought it would earn him a few coins. Still, the local was pleasant and eager to please, and he hadn't tipped Pascoe or his expensive equipment into the water…*yet*.

Pascoe raised his head from the camera and squinted at a dark shape in the distance. "Guide, what's that?"

"That? Yes, yes," Guide said, misunderstanding and directing the boat toward the dark shape. Pascoe sighed but didn't bother trying to explain himself. As the craft drew closer, weaving through the thin, drooping trees, Pascoe saw it was a structure made from rocks, almost like a small mountain rising out of the water. *Perhaps there's a system of caves running through it? That would make excellent film.*

Pascoe waved his guide to the left and felt a thrill at the sight of the cave opening not far ahead. Its dark rock arched high above the water and was filled with stalactites.

The audiences will love this. I could even claim this was the Diagen's home and that I encountered the fearsome beast in the darkness.

"Inside," he told Guide, and bent behind his camera to direct its lens over the rock formations and glistening stone. A steady wind blew through the caves, ruffling Pascoe's hair and drying the sweat on his face. He knew that meant the caves likely continued for a long way and probably had another opening farther into the water systems. They wouldn't be able to travel that far, though; the camera could only capture film when there was a certain amount of light. Pascoe had brought a large lamp, but even that wouldn't be strong enough to penetrate the repressive darkness.

Pascoe let the boat drift deeper into the cave, going farther than he knew the camera would capture. His curiosity was gaining on him, and he raised his head in wonder as he gazed at the moss-coated stalactites and stalagmites. The wind blew tiny insects into his face, but he hardly cared.

Guide gasped sharply then yelled something in his native language.

Pascoe turned toward him. "What's the matter with you?"

The short man was gesticulating wildly and speaking in broken English. "Sir! Sir! Air! Big air, comes fast here, goes fast there!"

"What on earth are you saying?" Pascoe leaned one arm on the side of the boat as he frowned.

Guide had lost his perpetual smile and was digging his pole into the water, trying to draw the boat back toward the exit.

Then the cause of his assistant's alarm struck Pascoe, and he turned back to the cave with mingled shock and incredulity.

The wind's direction had changed. When they'd entered the caves, it had been coming from deep inside the tunnel. But while he'd been engrossed in examining the walls, it had changed to blowing in from the outside. *Almost like…*

"Breathing." Pascoe turned toward the cave's entrance and saw the stalactites—*no*, he corrected himself, *the teeth*—descend to block out the light.

BUNKER

JAMES FROWNED AS HE POKED THE TIP OF HIS WALKING STICK into the soft ground. The last thing he'd been expecting to see in the vast Murrambungee National Park was concrete.

He'd gone off-trail to get a closer look at a huge gumtree that had been half-strangled in vines, and from there, it had been all too easy to follow a trail of small blue flowers farther into the forest. When he'd pushed through the thick vegetation and into a glade, James had been hoping for a natural clearing or possibly even a spring. Instead, he found something that definitely didn't belong so far from civilization.

The concrete stood a little higher than his head and rose from the ground at an angle, like a misplaced art exhibit. James approached the shape and stepped around it carefully. He quickly realized why the structure was sloped: on the other side, which was straight and horizontal, was a door. *It's a stairwell, then. But to where?*

James glanced back the way he'd come. He could still just barely see the vine-choked gumtree, but he was a good way off the regular trail. The stairwell's builder had apparently wanted it to stay hidden. And judging by the moss growing across the door's handle, that was exactly what had happened.

James didn't expect it to open, but he tried the door, anyway. The plain metal handle felt cold and slimy. He gave it a tug and was surprised to find the door hadn't been locked. It was gummed in place after years of neglect, but he was able to worm it open a crack with a few good pulls.

Stale, repulsive air came through the gap. It carried undertones of rot and death, and James pressed the back of his sleeve across his nose to block out the smell. *What on earth is this place?*

James didn't have a flashlight, but he'd brought a camera with a flash, so he raised it to the narrow opening and took a picture of the inside. The photo flashed up on his camera, and he saw stained concrete walls and dirty concrete stairs leading downward. The angle was bad, though, and he couldn't see the stairs' end. *Is it some sort of military bunker, maybe?*

James pocketed the camera and pulled on the door again, trying to widen the gap. Dirt and organic debris had built up around the doorframe, but it ground open slowly. Once the opening was barely wide enough for a human to fit through, James stepped back, panting, and held his camera inside for another photo.

The new picture was a little clearer, though his efforts to open the door had stirred up long-still dust, which became white blobs in the flash. The stairs continued for what seemed like a long way. Clearly, no one had ventured through the door in many years—possibly even decades. James cast a final glance in the direction of his trail then slipped through the narrow doorway.

The noises inside were magnified so that James's footsteps sounded like echoing thunder, no matter how carefully he placed them. He stuck to the left wall and ran his hand across the cold concrete as he followed the stairs. The narrow band of light from the outside world didn't penetrate far into the blackness, so after a dozen steps, James took another photo. It showed twenty stairs more, then a landing.

As he moved deeper, James tried to guess how far down the structure went. *I'd have to be well under the forest by now. Possibly even under the tree roots.*

The air chilled, and he was shivering by the time he reached the landing. Rounding the corner, he saw the stairs continued. He shook his head, dumbfounded, as he took another photo of the new stairwell. The disturbed dust was too thick for him to see any sort of end, though.

What the hell is this place?

James's heavy breathing mingled with the echoes of his footsteps as he followed the stairs deep underground. He paused every five or six paces to take a new photo and ensure he wasn't about to walk into a wall or fall off the edge of a drop-off. At last, after more than a hundred steps, the path leveled out into a corridor.

James took a photo and examined it, struggling to see through the floating dust. The stark concrete walls were bare except for dark shapes set into where the walls met the floor. James knelt, took another photo, and found the dark shapes were actually grates. They seemed to open into an even deeper area, though he couldn't see inside. *Sewerage, maybe? Or ventilation?* The grates were spaced ten feet apart, and James tried to count them as he moved through the hallway. With only his camera to show him the way, it was easy to become disoriented and lose track of how far he'd come, but he'd passed at least twenty of the grates before the hallway ended.

James, confused, stared at the photo of the empty wall in front of him. There was no door. There was no anything. The hallway simply ended, as though it had no greater purpose than to exist. James turned and took a photo of the length of the hallway, but he'd disturbed too much dust on his trip down, and couldn't make out anything except a blur of white.

As he retraced his path up the hallway, James kept one hand on the wall while he held the camera in the other and skimmed through the photos he'd taken. He was cold and eager to get back outside, but as he neared the halfway mark of the hallway, he stopped.

One of the pictures—one he'd taken to check he wasn't about to walk into anything—had focused on the walls rather than the dust motes, and it showed the grates a little more clearly than the other images had. And in one of the grates was…

No, that can't be possible. But it looks so much like a face…

James gasped as the bone-thin fingers, having slipped through the grate, fastened around his ankle and pulled.

SKIN HOUSE

COLD SKIN CARESSED RON AWAKE. HE GLANCED TOWARD THE mottled hand draped across the pillow, squeezed his eyes closed, and rolled away from it. The fingers twitched, seemingly beckoning him back.

He dipped his feet over the edge of the bed. Something scraped his toes as he slid them inside his slippers, and he recoiled with a barely muffled gasp. He turned the shoes over, and a dozen human molars clattered to the floor. Some rolled under the bed; others glittered on the polished wood. He considered not wearing the slippers then resolutely pulled them over his feet and went to the bathroom.

If you relent, you lose.

Three human fingers lay in the toothbrush holder. He ignored them as he took out his brush, even though one of them curled over at his touch. Ron watched his own face as he scrubbed his teeth. Human skin had been stretched over the wall behind him, and it pulsed from the effects of a nonexistent heart, but he didn't stare at it.

If you give it attention, you lose.

The shower had hair tangled in its showerhead. He tried pulling it free, but it had been woven through the tiny holes and refused to come out. Showering would still be possible, but it would mean letting the long, wet curls brush across his back. It was too much, even for him. He dressed and went downstairs.

A human head stared at him from the second shelf of his fridge. It had been there the day before, too, and the mottled skin seemed to be puckering from where the refrigerated air was drying it. The blanched-white eyes twitched to follow his movements as he retrieved leftover pizza. The flesh was blackening around the severed neck, and rotting fluid seeped from its open mouth, but he ignored it.

He knew what was happening. It had happened to his mother, too. She'd been consigned to the madhouse before his eighth birthday, where she incessantly screamed about her blankets being made of human flesh and fingernails scratching over her legs as she sat in her chair.

Insanity. If you give in to it, you lose. You go to the madhouse. You scream until you die.

Ron sat at the small kitchen table and ate his pizza. A dismembered tongue rested among the stack of unopened letters, its moisture soaking into and discoloring the paper.

Unlike his mother, he was holding it together. He'd inherited her insanity, but he'd learned from her mistakes, too. He wouldn't go shrieking to his neighbors about human body parts littering his home. As long as he kept his experiences to himself, the men in white coats would have no reason to visit.

Will it eventually go away, or will it be like this forever? Something wet dripped onto his hand. He refused to look toward the ceiling; he didn't want to see what was seeping onto him. Instead, he dried his fingers on a tissue and shifted the chair a foot to the left. *I'm not sure how long I can keep this up.*

It had started a week previously, when he'd found a severed toe on his living room floor. He'd almost called the police over it, except the toe had twitched. That clue had told him it was all in his head. If he called the police, they would come, and when he pointed at the twitching member, they would see nothing. And so he had to keep quiet about it. He had to ignore the steadily growing collection of human parts appearing around his home, to not let anyone suspect that he was cracking apart inch by inch.

It was Monday. He would need to be at the school in an hour to welcome his class. The previous Friday, just before leaving for the day, he'd found an ear in his drawer. He'd managed to squash any reaction that would alert his students, but he was dreading what he might find there that morning.

How bad will it get? There's more of it every day. Will my home eventually turn into nothing but an unholy collection of human fragments?

He shook his head and closed his eyes. *No. These images, these smells, these sensations—they're all in your head. They're not real, no matter how real they seem. You can endure. Just don't crack. Don't let anyone know.*

Faint, singsong chimes ran through the hallway. Ron stood and turned toward the door. He could see a uniformed figure through the frosted glass. A delivery man, young and cradling a parcel, waited outside.

Stay calm. Stay normal. Ron approached the door then recoiled as his feet landed in something soft. The skin from a human's torso was draped over the hallway runner. He'd squashed it just above the bellybutton.

It took immense willpower not to make a noise. He kept moving, stepping over the flesh and reaching for the doorhandle. *Smile, Ron,* he coached himself and exposed his teeth as he pulled open the door.

"Mr. Killborn?" the delivery man asked, holding out his clipboard. "A parcel for… What the hell?"

Ron followed the man's gaze. He was looking inside the apartment, his jaw slack and his eyes bulging, as he stared at the pulsing flesh covering the carpet.

"Oh," Ron said, uncertain whether to laugh or cry. "Do you see it, too?"

ABANDONED

FROM A DISTANCE, THE COLLAPSED TENT LOOKED ALMOST IDENTICAL to the dark rocks dotting the snow-blanketed slope. Angus didn't notice the flapping canvas until he was nearly on top of it.

Angus paused, his walking stick raised in preparation for his next step, and stared at the structure. Mount Onglavia wasn't a popular mountain-climbing destination, so he hadn't expected to see anyone else on his weekend trip.

The tent had collapsed and become half-buried by the snow, which didn't bode well for its occupant. Angus wasn't high enough for altitude sickness to be a serious concern, but there were still a multitude of other hazards that could maim or kill an unprepared climber. Angus quickened his pace, struggling through the knee-deep snow to reach the tent. "Hello?" he bellowed as he neared it, even though he didn't expect any answer. "Anyone hurt?"

Silence. Angus circled around the tent before drawing closer and tugging on the canvas. To his shock, the fabric pulled away in a thin strip. Something had sliced through the tent's walls, and only the poles and the weight of the snow held the remainder of the structure together.

What's strong enough to cut through this? Angus examined the frayed edges of the thick cloth. *A knife could do it. Or maybe a bear…except there aren't supposed to be bears around here.*

Angus pulled on the fabric, throwing off the heavy layer of snow to see underneath. Any thought that the tent might have been abandoned due to a defect left him. Inside was fully stocked with food, spare clothes, and hiking equipment.

Angus turned back to survey the harsh white landscape. The pine trees, spindly and dark green, were the only life he could see. The average climber would take more than a day to reach the mountain's base from Angus's current location. *Whoever owned the tent surely wouldn't have gone down without his supplies, would he?*

A knapsack sat in the corner, nestled in the snow but still full of clothes and equipment. Angus swiped his gloved hand through the white powder coating the tent's floor and found the sleeping bag underneath.

Angus didn't like to think about what had happened to the tent's owner. Mountaineering was a dangerous hobby, especially when done solo. Angus cast his eyes across the hills, wondering if the mystery climber's body was out there somewhere. The tent wasn't completely buried, which meant it must have been set up only a few days before.

Still, a few days is a long time for someone to survive around here.

The strangest part, though, were the slashed tent walls. Angus lifted parts of the canvas to examine the long, jagged gashes. He couldn't come up with any rational explanation for the damage.

A gust of wind blew a thin flurry of snow across the landscape and batted it against Angus's hooded face. With the wind came a low, drawn-out moan.

Angus turned toward the noise. He'd never heard anything like it before, but it somehow seemed to fit the bleak environment. He guessed it might have come from air being forced through a hole in a rock or possibly even a cave. It might have been some sort of wolf, though it sounded like no animal he'd ever heard before. The noise set his teeth on edge.

Angus lurched to his feet and pulled the walking stick from where he'd propped it in the snow. *I'll tell someone about the tent when I get back to base. They'll have a challenge finding a body among these rocks, but if someone's been reported missing, it might be a little comfort to their family to know their last location.*

Angus readjusted his balaclava and turned to the path that led toward the mountain's top. The summit was no more than four hours away—three, if the weather stayed good.

The low, long moan echoed across the icy hills again, and Angus paused. *No, don't start thinking that. Just keep walking.*

He turned back to the woods, his eyes scanning the trees. *But what if? What if it's the camper, hurt and calling for help?*

Angus shook his head and swiveled back to the path. *The tent's been abandoned for days. No one can survive out here without shelter for that long.*

Are you certain, though? Are you willing to risk leaving a man to die up here if you're wrong?

Angus turned back to the trees as he tried to figure out where the sound had come from. "Hello?"

C'mon. You're building things out of proportion. And the sun's getting low. You'll need to keep moving if you want to reach the top of the mountain before sundown.

Still, Angus hesitated. The noise came to him again, floating along the frigid air, its tone hollow, hungry, and raw.

Angus swore and began jogging toward the woods. He had difficulty moving through the snow at a normal rate; running was nearly impossible. Even so, the sound was fading, and he wanted to find its source before he lost it again.

He squirmed around an outcrop of rocks, and when he dropped into the sheltered hollow behind it, his foot landed on something that snapped under his weight. Angus felt his mouth dry. He stumbled backward, lost his balance, and fell.

Coiled into the sheltered hollow of the rocks was a human body, its limbs spread out and head lolled to one side. Angus recognized a popular brand of hiking jacket, though it had been unzipped to expose the belly underneath. Or what had once been the hiker's belly.

The body had been eviscerated, its clothing shredded and its insides torn out. The organs were frozen solid on the ground, waiting for spring to thaw the snow and make them vulnerable to birds of prey and wild beasts. The face, perfectly preserved, held an expression of mingled shock and horror. The eyes bulged, and the mouth was open, though something seemed to have eaten its tongue.

The wail came from the patch of woods behind Angus, and it sounded far, far closer than it had before. He turned slowly and faced the being that watched him from just behind the closest trees.

RADIO

THE CAR HORN BLARED, CUTTING THROUGH LUKE'S MOMENTARY distraction. He corrected his pickup truck and refocused on the narrow, twisting band of road as the car passed him in the opposite direction.

The twenty-minute drive through the mountain pass always left Luke jumpy. A high rock wall rose on his left side, where small sickly plants struggled to dig their roots into the granite. To his right was a drop-off, separated from the road by a thin metal rail.

Everyone, including Luke, took the mountain pass too quickly. The speed sign said sixty kilometers an hour, but he pushed the car to seventy-five. *The faster I get to the other side, the better.*

Moonlight, bright thanks to the full orb, flooded the road. It was well past midnight, and exhaustion was gnawing at Luke. All he wanted was to get to his friend's house, roll onto the couch he'd been promised, and sleep until midday the next morning.

The car's left wheels vibrated as they ran over the gravel lining the edge of the road. Luke swore and corrected his path again. *I'm getting sloppy. We can't have that.*

He pressed his palm to the radio's button, and the jovial voice of a talk-show host filled the car. *Prerecorded,* Luke thought, based on how buzzed the man's voice sounded. No one was that perky at one in the morning.

The noise helped, though, and Luke let it wash over him as he focused his eyes on the road. For some reason, there was a second voice in the background of the station, talking a little too quietly for Luke to make out the words.

Did they mess up the recording, or something? Maybe they're playing two tracks at the same time.

It was both frustrating and distracting, and Luke changed the station. The new wavelength had party music, which they always seemed to play on Fridays. It wasn't his kind of tune, but beggars couldn't be choosers.

There was something off about the songs, though, and it took Luke a moment to realize what it was. A man's voice in the background was throwing off the beat.

That's the same voice that was on the other station. Maybe my radio's picking up interference?

Luke scanned through four other stations, and each time, the voice came through, too faint to hear the words, but not quiet enough to ignore. Luke scowled at the radio, trying to figure out what was wrong with it, and a blaring car horn shocked him back to alertness.

Jeez, don't lose focus now. There's only ten more minutes on this road, then you're back into the farmland. Pay attention.

He'd left the radio on a dead space between stations. Strangely, though, the voice continued through the crackling static. Without other voices or music to distract him, Luke tried to make out the words.

"…eighteen dead…found…from the wreckage…"

Okay, so it's a news station, then. Luke reached out to turn off the radio, but then the static cleared, and the voice became clear.

"A private plane was shot out of the sky by Kyle King, who had drunkenly mistaken it for a large bird. The plane's pilot, Tom Jenner, died instantly. In Wisconsin, USA, Aubrey Childs covered her heater with a blanket before going to bed, which started a fire while she and her family were asleep. All three died from smoke inhalation. Jon and Louise Redcliffe went scuba diving during their honeymoon in Bali. Louise's equipment malfunctioned, drowning her before she could reach the surface. In the West Isles…"

The hairs rose across the back of Luke's arms. It was nothing like any news station he'd heard before. The announcer's voice was unnervingly even and lacked any sort of nuance or emotion. The man sounded almost as though he were listing facts from a card. The deaths, a constant stream of them, seemed to have no relationship to each other. They spanned from Iceland to New Zealand and had a multitude of causes.

"In Cannes, Australia, Greg Favetta suffered a heart attack at his granddaughter's birthday party. The guests assumed it was a joke and only called an ambulance when it was too late to save him. In Vanuatu, a…"

Luke hit the radio's button, silencing it. *What a weird station. Maybe it's a private project. Like some local got his hands on a radio broadcaster and is doing this as a sick joke or something.*

The radio crackled, and the monotonous voice filled Luke's car again. "In New York, USA, three teenagers were shot in an alley by their classmate, Kendrick Heslop. Kendrick then turned the gun on himself. In Denmark, Faye Broger choked on a fish bone. She lived alone and won't be found for five days."

Wait…won't be found?

Luke slammed his fist on the dash. Static filled the radio for a second but couldn't smother the unrelenting voice. Luke tried pressing the power button multiple times, but nothing stopped the monologue.

"What the hell?" Luke spat.

"In Western Vale, Australia, Antonio Reynolds lost control of his vehicle while navigating a narrow mountain pass. He hit a pickup truck belonging to Luke Guerra. Both died instantly."

Luke turned his eyes back to the road and gasped.

WAX MUSEUM

As Jared pulled his car into one of the dozens of empty parking spots, it was hard not to stare at the garish sign hung on the building ahead. *Fat Clifford's Fantastic Wax Sculptures*, painted in bright carnival colors and exaggerated letters, seemed strangely irreverent that evening. Dark clouds had gathered to cover the moon, and a freezing wind tugged at Jared's coat as he left the car and approached the staff entrance at the back of the building.

A tall, pinch-nosed woman was waiting for him inside. She exhaled audibly as he entered, then grabbed his sleeve and pulled him farther into the building. "You're the new guard, aren't you? Thank goodness. My daughter's birthday dinner is tonight, and I'm already late for it."

"Oh, sorry—I thought I was on time—"

"You are. Here, keys to the building. I'll show you the security booth. You've done night guard work before, right?"

Jared hesitated only a fraction of a second. "Oh, yeah." In truth, it was his first time. He'd been surprised by how fast the process was; he'd applied that morning, had a phone interview in the afternoon, and been told to show up at ten o'clock that night. He wasn't about to complain, though. His rent was three weeks overdue, and he would have shoveled trash if anyone had been hiring for it.

"Here." The woman—Simone, according to her name tag—ushered him into a small booth. Eight screens with black-and-white feed were set above a simple desk. "Did Clifford explain the job to you?"

"Um—" The interview had been so fast that Jared had barely gotten the address. "Watch the building?"

"That's it in a nutshell." She pointed to the screens. "These wax sculptures are incredibly expensive; keep an eye on them to make sure no one breaks in to steal or damage them. Watch the screens, and once an hour, walk through the building. Those are Clifford's express instructions. The screens capture most of the rooms, but the hourly walk-through is very important to double-check everything is fine."

"And, um"—Jared adjusted his tie, which suddenly felt too tight—"what happens if it's not?"

Simone blinked at him. "Then you fix it."

"Uh…"

"Look, I've got to go. I'm so late. You'll be fine. Just do the walk-through every hour and watch the screens. It's a stupidly simple job."

Jared continued to fiddle with his tie as he listened to her footsteps fade and the metal staff entrance door slam.

Just like the interview, his introduction to the job had happened so quickly that he felt as if he were trying to correct his balance on a constantly rocking boat. He stood in the booth for a few moments, half expecting someone would come back and give him a proper job description, then sighed and rubbed his hands through his hair.

"It's cool. It's a stupidly easy job, like she said. You'll be fine."

A flashlight stood on the desk by the screens, and Jared picked it up. He searched through the drawers in case he'd also been given a weapon, but there was no such luck. All that remained was a stick of gum, probably left there by the last guard.

Without anything else to do, Jared turned on the flashlight and left the booth for his first walk-through. It didn't take long for him to become hopelessly lost.

Should've turned the lights on, he thought bitterly as he found himself at a dead end. However, Simone hadn't shown him where the switches were, and his narrow beam of light showed him only tiny slices of the space with each step.

The wax museum was larger than he'd expected. At least a dozen rooms held countless wax figures, eerily lifelike and horribly plastic. He passed celebrities, historical figures, and even book characters. Every time he turned his flashlight, a new face was staring at him, fake eyes, hair, and smiles catching in the beam.

Cold sweat trickled down Jared's back. During the interview, he'd been told the previous night guard had quit without notice, and he was starting to understand why. If he hadn't been desperate for the money, he would have walked out right then.

As he continued farther into the house of shadowed, awkwardly posed models, he somehow found himself in a room of deformed figures. Their heads lolled at awkward angles, some were missing limbs, and others were partially melted. They had been arranged along the walls, all facing the door, their twisted visages enough to make Jared feel faintly sick.

Suspecting the room wasn't part of the public tour, he backed out of the room. The glassy eyes and lopsided smiles followed him until he closed the door.

It was an immeasurable relief when he caught sight of light coming from below the booth's door. He hurried to it and locked himself inside. The tie still felt too tight, so he loosened it some more then pressed a hand over his heart.

The guard's booth was small, but at least it was brightly lit. Jared slumped into the chair behind the desk and ran his hands over his face. He guessed the wax museum must be charming and interesting by day, when the lights were on and the signs were easy to read. At night, though, it had turned into something out of his worst nightmares. Jared was glad to be away from it.

Well…mostly away from it. The eight screens showed several of the horrific scenes in black-and-white night vision. For some reason, one of the cameras was pointed toward the storage room holding the deformed sculptures. Their eyes shone white through the camera, the way an animal's flash in the light.

The chills wouldn't abate. Jared got to his feet, felt behind the screens, and pulled the plug he found there. The images disappeared in a faint whine, and the empty black was a relief in comparison.

I'll look for another job, Jared promised himself as he lolled back in the chair. *As soon as I get one, I can ditch this place. Maybe I just won't turn up one day, like that last chap. I don't know why this place even needs a security guard at night, anyway...and the hourly walk-throughs feel pointless. What can my presence achieve that a cheap motion sensor won't do more efficiently and for a fraction of the price?*

Time seemed to crawl by. Jared had brought a novel, but he didn't feel like reading. Instead, he leaned back in the chair, folded his arms, and closed his eyes in an attempt to relax.

He started awake sometime later. It took him a moment to remember where he was, then he checked his watch. It was nearly four in the morning. His shift would only last for two more hours.

His first emotion was guilt at failing to do what had been described as a "stupidly simple" job. His second was gratitude that he'd woken before his negligence could be discovered. He sat up in the chair and groaned as a pinched nerve in his neck made itself felt.

Scccrrrthhh...scccrrrthhh...

Jared snapped his attention toward the booth's door. Something was scratching at its outside. His heart skipped a beat as he half rose out of the seat.

Scccrrrthhh...scccrrrthhh...

He mouthed a swearword as panic hit. Jared scrambled for

the back of the monitor system and replugged it. All eight screens blinked for a second then resumed their feed. He scanned them, but none of them showed the hallway outside the security booth.

Scccrrrthhh…scccrrrthhh…

"Crap!"

His nerves were hot. There was no phone inside the booth, and he'd left his cell phone at home. There was no way to contact the outside world without leaving. Jared lifted his flashlight, base turned outward to use as a bludgeon, and prepared to turn the handle. He held a small hope that it might be a prank, a welcome-to-the-job hazing, but he was fully prepared to slam the door closed if it was anything else.

Scccrrrthhh…

He swung the door open, and the scraping fell silent. Outside the room stood a tall sculpture of a woman in a historical dress, her eyes directed toward Jared's face, her smile unnaturally wide. She was motionless, but her fingers were still extended, their strangely realistic nails held in the exact place they would need to be to scratch at the booth's door.

Jared ran. His flashlight beam jittered over walls, floors, and countless leering wax figures. They'd moved, he was sure. They no longer stood on their pedestals, but blocked the walkways. Jared ducked and wove about them, his heart ready to explode, and was certain he could hear shuffling footsteps behind him.

The building was a maze, and he could have cried his relief when he recognized the hallway to the staff entrance. He burst through the metal door, dashed down the four steps to the parking lot, and threw himself into the only remaining vehicle—his car.

As he turned toward the area's exit, he saw a man blocking the road. Jared slowed the car as he neared, and he realized the shape in the harsh beams of his headlights wasn't flesh and blood, as he'd first thought, but a wax figure. The man was tall and wide set, wearing a blue coat; hands planted on hips, beady eyes staring unwaveringly at the car. A big name tag on his lapel read Fat Clifford.

Jared had let the car come to a halt. A quiet click was all the warning he had that the passenger door had been opened; he looked to his side, where one of the deformed melted mannequins was halfway into his car, a contorted hand stretched toward Jared's tie.

Without hesitation, he hit the accelerator. The car jerked forward, throwing the reaching wax figure out, and screeched toward Fat Clifford. The statue's wild smile didn't falter as the car hit it, knocked it down, and bounced over it.

Jared sucked in thin, terrified breaths. He kept both feet pressed to the accelerator as he urged the car to take him as far from *Fat Clifford's Fantastic Wax Sculptures* as possible.

BOGROT

MEG FISHED THROUGH HER PURSE. "HE WASN'T ANY TROUBLE, was he?"

Tara, her schoolbooks tucked under one arm, shook her head so vigorously that her hair fluttered around her face. "Nah. He went to bed early and hasn't stirred since."

"Good." Meg produced the promised twenty dollars and added an extra five. She'd been away for nearly an hour longer than she'd anticipated; she could only be grateful that Tara was patient enough to wait for her.

Tara said her goodbyes and hurried to her car while Meg let herself into the house. The building was still and dark. Meg didn't expect her husband home for another hour or two; it was football night for him, and sometimes, he wouldn't come home until the early morning, tired and delighted, smelling of cheap beer.

Meg dropped her car keys and purse onto the kitchen counter

then went to her son's room. She kept the hall light off and pressed the door open gently, expecting Riley to be asleep. The boy was sitting bolt upright in his bed, though, and he gasped when Meg opened the door.

She turned on the light and went to him. "Hey, honey. What's wrong?"

His dark eyes, so much like his father's, blinked at her from under long lashes. "Bad dream." His eyes immediately turned to the window.

"Want to tell me about it?" Meg asked, sitting on the edge of his bed. She could hear their dog, Jasper, barking in the yard. *Something's gotten him worked up. I'll have to check on him before bed.*

Riley gave his mother a sidelong glance but hesitated, seemingly uncertain how to start. "Have you ever heard of the Bogrot?"

Meg quirked her eyebrows up. "Nope. What's that?"

"Tara was telling me about them." Riley shrugged and pulled the blankets farther up his body. "She says one's been following her."

Meg pursed her lips. "She shouldn't be telling you scary stories, especially not before bedtime."

Riley's huge eyes turned back to Meg, desperately sincere in his desire not to get his babysitter in trouble. "Don't blame Tara. I made her! I begged her and begged her to tell me the scariest story she could. She didn't really want to, but I made her tell me about the Bogrot."

Bogrot sounded like exactly the sort of name a young adult would choose for a fictional monster. Meg sighed. "Okay, why don't you tell me about this Bogrot, and I'll tell you if I think it's scary."

Riley shrugged. She could tell he was trying to look nonchalant, but the way his eyes kept flicking to the window gave him away. "Well…" he said, speaking slowly. "She said there was a monster, which she called the Bogrot, that used to follow her around at night. She didn't like going outside after dark because of it."

Meg followed her son's eyes to the window, where the moonlight pierced the thick trees at the back of the yard. Jasper's barking was becoming more frantic. *He's probably found a raccoon.* "And what exactly does a Bogrot do?"

"It makes squelching noises when it follows her. She says it hides in the shadows so it's hard to see, but it has yellow eyes and really long claws."

That sounds ridiculous. He's getting too old to be frightened of monsters. "And it scared you so badly, you had a nightmare?"

Riley bristled. "You didn't hear the way she described it! Like it could really be there, waiting for me to step outside. Waiting for *you*." He shivered and pulled his blankets still higher. "And I thought I heard you call Jasper from the back of the garden, and Jasper was barking and barking and barking, and then suddenly there was a snap of huge teeth, and…" Riley turned his huge eyes toward his mother.

Meg felt a stab of guilt for teasing her son. *Of course an eight-year-old would be disturbed if he dreamed his pet had been eaten.* She pulled Riley into a hug and squeezed him tightly. "Hey, it's okay. The Bogrot didn't get Jasper. You can hear him barking, can't you? He's fine."

"Yeah," Riley said, though he didn't sound convinced. "It seemed so real, though."

"It can't have been, honey." Meg brushed Riley's golden-blond hair out of his face and kissed his forehead. "I only just got home. There's no way I could have been calling Jasper."

Riley hesitated, and Meg guessed she wasn't getting the full story. She raised her eyebrows at him in silent question, and he shrugged. "It's just the other thing Tara said. She said the Bogrot can imitate human voices. So it could have been the Bogrot at the back of the yard, calling Jasper. And he thought it was you, and…" Riley shook his head and squeezed his eyes closed. "Never mind. I don't want to think about it."

Meg sighed. She had no idea what Tara had been thinking, coming up with such a ghastly story. The only comfort was Jasper's persistent barking. Meg gave her son's forehead a kiss then stood and approached the window. The clear moonlight painted over the closer patches of grass, but the trees filled the back of the yard with shadows. A glint of silver caught Meg's eyes, and she saw a dog tag lying on the ground next to…

Fur. A clump of fur, golden-brown with bloodstained tips, lay next to Jasper's tag.

Meg raised her eyes, searching the yard for the barking dog, and saw two faintly glowing globes hidden in the shadows at the back of the yard. Then the globes blinked as the Bogrot barked, and barked, and barked.

BEANIE'S FAST FOOD

BEANIE'S PLASTIC EYES SURVEYED THE RESTAURANT AS HIS WIDE smile stretched his rosy cheeks. Paulie always made a point of tapping the bright-yellow button on Beanie's suit whenever he passed, as though the giant plastic torso could bring him good luck. He did so then as he crossed to the door at the back of the restaurant, two garbage bags clenched in his other fist.

He could hear Jen, Paulie's coworker, grumbling as she sorted the inventory in the walk-in fridge. She hated the closing shift almost as much as Paulie did. He shoved through the narrow door at the back of the building and used one foot to slow its closing so that it would hit the latch but not lock.

The cold night air bit at his face and ears. He jogged toward the dumpsters at the opposite side of the parking lot, trying to keep up his momentum and reminding himself that he would be home in another twenty minutes.

Paulie was halfway across the parking lot when a bang startled him. He turned, surveying the nearby streets, which were empty. The parking lot had only three cars: his, Jen's, and another he didn't recognize. The car possibly belonged to a druggie or a drunk who'd forgotten where he'd parked. It had happened before.

Their branch of Beanie's Fast Food was nestled on the edge of a not-so-pleasant part of town. Train lines ran behind the parking lot, and every half an hour, a carriage would whistle past, drowning out their customer's voices. The slums on the other side of the tracks housed some of the strangest people Paulie had ever met—and he'd met his fair share of weirdos. He couldn't count the number of employees his boss, Glenn, had fired, and for far more extreme reasons than he'd ever anticipated. Selling drugs over the counter was a common one, but two cooks had been let go for trying to deep fry a rat, and one employee had tried to gouge out a customer's eye. Some days, Paulie felt as if he, Jen, and Glenn were the only sane people left in the world.

Paulie pushed the dumpster's lid open and threw the bags inside. *Nearly the end of your shift, buddy,* he reminded himself as he turned back to the store's sooty back entrance. *Then you get to enjoy opening shift tomorrow, too. Hooray.*

The streetlamps spaced around the parking lot left stark circles of light on the black asphalt. Paulie didn't like walking through them and skirted around their edges, eager to get inside the relatively warm eatery.

He hesitated at the door. It was pulled tightly closed. *Must have been the wind. That could have been what the slamming noise was; the door being forced closed.*

Muttering under his breath, Paulie unlocked the door and pushed inside. The back areas were far less orderly and clean than they kept the parts of the kitchen visible to the public, but, between himself and Jen, they managed to stop it from getting too disgusting. Paulie could still hear Jen in the walk-in fridge, muttering to herself as she counted off inventory and made a list for Glenn to reorder goods the following morning.

Paulie grabbed the broom from the corner of the room and returned to the front of the store, where the floor was permanently in need of cleaning. He raised a hand to tap Beanie's bright-yellow button out of habit then pulled his hand back as he touched something wet.

"What the hell…?"

A red substance had been smeared across the plastic mascot's neck, connecting one ear to the other in a gory replica of a cut throat. The substance had dribbled over the torso, including the button Paulie liked to tap.

Paulie's mouth felt dry. He stared at the mascot, too confused to feel proper shock. *I was only outside for a couple of minutes. Who could have done this? Not Jen, surely?*

As if on cue, Jen rounded the corner and stopped short at the sight of the defaced statue. Her eyes roved from the red splatter to Paulie's tinted fingertips, and a scowl settled above her dark eyes. "What the hell, Paulie?"

The shocked indignation in her voice convinced Paulie that she had no knowledge of the vandalism. That was enough to shake him out of his stupor, and he took a step back, feeling revolted.

"Wasn't me," he said. He pressed his thumb against the red liquid on his index finger, trying to guess its origin based on its viscousness. As he rubbed his fingers together, the substance began to dry and tack in the way only one thing could. "Blood…"

"Don't be an ass," Jen snapped, moving closer to the mascot. She squinted at the stains, seeming reluctant to touch them. "I mean, it looks like it, but…"

"I thought I heard the door slam," Paulie said, as the memory came back to him. "When I was taking the trash out."

"That wasn't you?" Jen's eyes scoured his face, testing his truthfulness, then she swore under her breath and pulled out her phone. "If this is really blood… Jeez. I'm calling Glenn. I'm not paid enough to deal with this sort of crap."

Paulie couldn't stop staring at the mascot. The blood had been smeared deliberately to replicate a cut throat. *Is that a threat? Who'd want to threaten us? Could be a dismissed employee, I guess, or maybe a customer who really hated their food…*

A strange haunting jingle came from farther in the store. Both Paulie and Jen swung toward it. From what Paulie could tell, its source was somewhere near the back of the dining room.

"It's the boss's phone," Jen said, taking her cell phone away from her ear and glancing about the shadowed eatery. "He's still here."

Paulie remembered the third car left beside his and Jen's in the parking lot. It had been too deep in the shadows to see clearly, but it could have been Glenn's.

"C'mon," Jen said, pushing past Paulie to cross the dining area. "I'm not going to stand for any sick pranks."

Her voice was strong, but he thought he detected a note of anxiety hidden in it. He followed her as the haunting jingle led them to the bathrooms at the back of the building.

The ringtone came from the men's room, and Jen pushed in without hesitation. "Glenn?" she called, and to her credit, she hesitated only a second before striding toward the stalls. "What the hell do you think you're playing at?"

Paulie froze in the doorway, his nerves on fire and the hair on his arms standing on end. Only one stall had its door closed: the last one in the row. It wasn't fully shut, though—the door had been pulled to, but not locked.

"Jen," Paulie said, and the word rasped across his dry lips. "Jen, don't."

She either ignored him or hadn't heard him. Just like she hadn't heard the dripping sound—barely audible above Glenn's ringtone—or seen the trickle of dark blood running from inside the stall and dribbling toward the drain.

Jen pushed open the stall door, and her scowl morphed into an expression of absolute terror.

99 MESSAGES

JUST INSIDE HIS APARTMENT'S FRONT DOOR, MIRKO DROPPED HIS suitcase on the floor and sighed. He took a moment to bask in the blissful silence and stretch the knots out of his back. Work had been grueling, and he was looking forward to running a hot bath and reheating the previous night's leftovers.

Mirko crossed the room to the sideboard and pressed the flashing button on his answering machine. He untied his shoes and kicked them off as he listened to the mechanical female voice.

"You have…ninety-nine…new messages."

Mirko hesitated, one foot raised, ready to pull off his sock. *Ninety-nine? That can't be right.*

"First new message received today at…eight…forty-six… a.m."

He'd left for work at eight forty-five on the dot. He must have just barely missed the call.

There were several seconds of silence, then a voice, oddly crackly, said, "Hello, Mirko. I'm going to start counting now. Are you ready?"

Both socks off, Mirko gave the answering machine his full attention. The voice was silent for nearly half a minute, then it said, calmly and precisely, "Ninety-nine."

The message bank beeped, and the mechanical voice returned. "Next new message received today at…eight…forty-nine… a.m."

Again, after a second of silence, the unfamiliar voice said, "Ninety-eight."

Mirko rubbed his thumbs into the corners of his eyes. *Is this some kind of joke?*

He didn't recognize the voice. It had no discernible accent, but spoke in an odd monotone lacking both inflection and emotion. He couldn't even tell if it belonged to a man or a woman. Crackles, as though the voice were speaking through a walkie-talkie, accompanied it.

"Next new message received today at…eight…fifty-two… a.m."

"Ninety-seven."

It's not seriously counting down from a hundred, is it? Mirko glanced at the number flashing on the side of his machine: ninety-six new messages. *How long would it have taken someone to record all of these?*

He mashed his thumb into the button on the side of the machine, deleting messages before they played. He watched the number of unheard messages drop from the nineties down to fifty, then twenty, then ten. Once he'd reached the third-to-last message, he released the button to let it play.

"Next new message received today at…twelve…eighteen…p.m."

"You forgot to lock your door this morning, Mirko. Three."

Mirko slowly turned toward the rear of his house. The hairs on the backs of his arms rose.

"Next new message received today at…twelve…twenty-one…p.m."

"Mirko, have you found a weapon yet? Two."

This is a joke. A sick, strange joke. Mirko turned back to the answering machine, where the number one flashed on the screen.

"Next new message received today at…twelve…twenty-five…p.m."

"Are you ready, Mirko? One."

A long, loud beep followed as the phone marked all messages listened to.

Mirko turned slowly, swallowing the dry taste in his mouth. For a moment, his apartment was filled with complete, perfect silence, then there was a quiet click as someone fastened the lock on his front door.

DEATH FOLLOWS

Death's exhale was a protracted, scraping rattle. It conjured memories of dead leaves skittering over dirt, fingernails drawing across gravestones, or an elderly man's final rasp.

It wasn't unfamiliar to John. He was at the head of his driveway, and it took a moment of searching to spot the black shadow nestled in the corner of his neighbor's house where the vines grew thick and the slanted roof blocked out most of the waning light.

The specter looked nearly identical to a shadow, save for its movements and the flash of light reflecting off its eyes. It was taller than a human, but its back and shoulders were stooped. Its unnaturally long fingers twitched at its side as it stared at John.

He turned, put his hands into his pockets, and began walking to town. His job as a spirit medium had introduced him to the specter. Curiosity in life after death, of spirits and lost souls, had increased dramatically at the turn of the century, and John's unique talents had allowed him to charge a rich sum for contacting the husbands, sons, and daughters of grieving women. The spirits would answer his call and communicate messages through taps, chills, and whispers.

John had been a spirit medium for close to a year when he first saw Death. During his work, he'd given a great deal of thought to the souls and where they went after their mortal bodies perished, but none to the entity that reaped them. Then, one evening, he'd glimpsed the shadow in the back of an elderly widow's parlor. Its lamp-like eyes were fixated on her bowed head, and a sense of unease had prickled at John's skin and made his saliva bitter. He'd left early. The following morning, he received word that the widow had passed in her sleep.

Since then, he'd seen Death lingering around men and women who were near the end of their time on earth. The creature was infallible. And this time, it had come for John.

He picked up his pace and heard the scrape of long, steady footsteps behind him. Death had seemingly endless patience, he'd learned. The intended victims would live hours or even days after the specter began trailing them.

That gives me time, he thought, though he didn't know what he intended to use that time for. His first thought was to settle his affairs, but he had no wife and no children to settle on. There was no one he cared about to say goodbye to. As a spirit medium, he traveled through towns so quickly that he never became attached to the inhabitants.

At the end of his lane, the road split. Left went toward

town; right led into the countryside. John paused, considering his options. He didn't dare turn around, but he could hear the specter coming closer, moving to stand in his shadow, to breathe its fetid, icy breath across the back of his neck.

He turned right. If he was going to die, he would do it in a discreet place where his body wouldn't cause too much distress. The forest, perhaps, or he could sit on the bridge over the river and hope to keel into the water and be swept away.

John was faintly surprised by his serenity in the face of his own death. He'd seen so much of it in the previous year of his life, had called up so many spirits, that mortality no longer held any horror for him. At least, not the kind of horror normal people tasted.

He was inevitably asked the same questions at each séance. *Does it hurt? Are you happy?* The replies were always comforting, but a theory had grown in John over his year of conducting séances. *If I were trapped in a realm of constant suffering, would I reveal that to my grieving wife when there is nothing she can do? Or would I lie, knowing that at least one of us would be happier for it?*

John wiped the back of his hand over his lips. The fingers were shaking. Death no longer followed at a safe distance, but stayed near enough to touch, those sickening rattles echoing in John's ear with every exhale.

He was tempted to bargain, but he already knew the creature was beyond reason. It wasn't the intelligent, scythe-carrying skeleton often portrayed in stories. Death was impassionate, uncaring, animalistic in its thoughts and intentions. No silver tongue could persuade the being away from its course.

The river wasn't far ahead. John had been hoping to sit on the edge of the railing while he waited, but to his frustration, he saw a man already stood there, leaning on the wood and watching the water below.

"'Lo!" the stranger called as John neared. He didn't see the extra shadow trailing John; no one ever saw it.

John gave a curt nod, intending to cross the bridge and find a quieter place to die, but the stranger turned toward him, a lopsided grin growing over his face.

"You're the medium, aren't you? My aunt had you for a séance last week."

"Ah—" John hated to stop when the specter was so close in his wake, but a strange thought occurred to him. He stopped next to the man, close to the edge of the river, and gave him a quick look-over. He was young, no more than twenty-five, and had dressed casually, probably planning to spend the day outdoors. "Do you have much interest in the next life?"

The man laughed and clapped John on the shoulder. "I intend no offense, understand, but I firmly believe your kind are charlatans, the lot of you."

John's smile was tighter than he would have liked it. He looked behind them; Death stood close, its bony, unnaturally long fingers raised to caress John's shoulder. The world seemed to lose color when he looked at the specter. For a moment, all he could see was the flash of light playing over its sightless eyes.

It's impulsive. Animalistic. I wonder...

He reached into his pocket. His companion had returned to

gazing over the edge of the bridge, teeth sparkling in the dull sunlight. "I'm sure your antics are good for an evening's entertainment, but I don't believe for a second you do anything more than comfort the grieving."

"You'll believe soon enough." John flipped the knife out effortlessly and drew it across the man's throat. A gush of red poured from the cut, and the man's smile finally disappeared into a horrified shriek.

John pressed his hand over the man's mouth, silencing him, as they watched his lifeblood drain into the river below. He spoke quickly, desperately. "I won't ask your forgiveness. But death expects a victim. Please, stand in my stead."

There was so much red, so much more than John had anticipated. His companion's eyes rolled back into his head, and the grabbing hands stilled and fell.

John let the man slump over the bridge's railing. Death no longer watched him, but the creature's mouth opened a fraction to reveal the flash of discolored teeth. It draped itself across the dying man and ate. John watched for a moment, sweat pouring down his face and his limbs, so unsteady that he was afraid he might collapse. Then he threw the knife into the river, skirted around the feeding shadow, and ran.

AFTER CLOSING

SOREN WOKE WITH A SNORT. HIS NECK HURT. THE PAIN RADIATED down his spine and into his left arm. He sat up, trying to figure out where he was, and bumped his head on something hard.

What...?

He glanced up and saw the underside of a scratched wooden desk. Familiar smells reached him then—paper, disinfectant, and the tang from the sickly sweets kept in a bowl on the help counter—and he remembered. *The library. I slipped under the desk to have a nap before going home. What time is it?*

Soren pushed the chair out of his way and crept out from under the counter. The lights were out, and the library was deathly quiet. He'd slept through closing, he realized, with a flush of mingled embarrassment and light anxiety.

There's got to be a way to open the doors from the inside, right? I won't be locked in here until morning, will I?

He got to his feet and cringed as pins and needles shot down his leg. He held still, one hand grasping the back of the chair, the other resting on the desk where his schoolbooks were still stacked, while he waited for the blood flow to return to the limb.

The librarians mustn't have checked the library very thoroughly before going home. I was well hidden under the desk, but there was no way they would have missed me if they'd tried to take my books.

A scratching sound drew Soren's attention. Something was moving near the back of the library. He frowned and crept forward to see around the nearby bookshelf. *There shouldn't be anyone else here, not at this time of night.*

As he leaned forward to see around the shelf, Soren caught a glimpse of a small figure crouched near the back of the room. It seemed to be digging through the small bin in the corner. Soren stared at it, mesmerized and unable to comprehend what he was seeing, as the figure's dexterous limbs moved. It was bone-thin and naked, and though it was hard to see with only the glow of the streetlights filtering through the library's window, he thought its skin was gray.

The being in the corner of the room suddenly stopped its rummaging. Its head swiveled, the neck spinning past a normal human's range, to face Soren. He caught a glimpse of red-pink eyes behind strands of long, greasy black hair, then he ducked out of sight and pressed his back to the shelf as his heart thundered in his ears.

What was that? It's not human, that's for sure.

He held his breath and listened. After a moment, the faint scratching sounds resumed. *Maybe it didn't see me. Maybe it's blind.*

Against his better judgment, Soren edged closer to the edge of the shelf and carefully extended his head forward to see the corner of the room. The bin was still there, but the creature had gone.

Soren's mouth dried as he pulled back again. Cold sweat built across his torso. *I've got to get out of here.*

He was near the back of the library. The entrance stood two dozen paces away, past the help desk. Soren, moving as quietly as he could, turned to grab his books.

The creature stood directly behind him, within touching distance, its huge red eyes framed in heavy shadows.

Soren froze. He opened his mouth—whether to speak or scream, he wasn't sure—but no noise escaped him.

The being's eyes narrowed, and it reached toward him. The fingers were far longer than they had any right to be, with at least five knuckles each. They ended in sharpened claws, and Soren felt as though his heart might explode as they stretched toward his face.

He jolted backward without realizing what he was doing and hit the library shelf. His feet skidded out from under him, and Soren grabbed at the shelves as he toppled to the ground. His weight was enough to pull the heavy structure free from its bolts and bring it crashing down on both him and the creature.

The books poured from the shelves as it fell, and Soren caught a half-second glimpse of fury blazing in the monster's face before it was smothered. The bookcase landed on Soren's leg, which was still numb from when he'd fallen asleep, and he grunted through his teeth.

Get up, idiot! Run!

Soren pulled his legs out from under the books, gained his feet, and staggered toward the library's door. He thought he could hear the skittering, clawing noise again, but when he turned, the room behind him was still except for the settling pile of books.

The library's doors had motion sensors to open them, but they'd been turned off at closing. Soren tried to wedge his fingertips into the gap between the doors and pull them open, but they wouldn't move.

There has to be a spare key or something.

Soren turned to put the doors at his back. He could see the fallen shelf's silhouette in the back of the room, but saw movement. *Is it still there, under the books? Did I kill it?*

Soren's breaths came as thin wheezes as he moved around the help desk and searched knickknacks hidden there. In the darkness, his hands brushed over paperclips, erasers, pencils, pens, letter holders, and a glass still half-full of water, without finding any keys.

He swore under his breath then fell still as he heard the noise again. *Like fingers brushing across paper.* He raised his head to look over the top of the help desk, but he couldn't see any sign of motion or of the red eyes. His lips formed another swearword, but he didn't dare speak it.

There's got to be keys. Got to be!

Soren turned to look at the wall behind the desk, and then he saw it: a door set between the shelves had been left open. It seemed to be some sort of storage closet, though Soren didn't remember ever seeing the library staff use it.

I'd be safe in there, I bet. I could barricade myself inside and wait until morning.

Without a second thought, Soren crossed the distance and stepped into the room, pulling the door closed behind himself. He fished his phone out of his pocket and turned it on to use its light. The glow was too dim to allow him to make out details, but what he could see made his heart freeze.

A cot had been set against one wall, with a bucket just below it. The cot had blankets and a pillow, but they were grimy with age. A single chair sat against the opposite wall, taking up the rest of the cramped room.

It…lives here? Why? How? Does one of the librarians own it and they let it out at night?

Soren backed up against the door, struggling to draw breath. *I can't stay here. Not in its home. I've got to get out. Even if I break the glass doors…I could use the chair…*

He opened the door a crack and edged out of the room, moving his feet in slow sweeps across the carpet to minimize noise, intent on the sliding glass doors.

The sound—that faint crackle of nails on paper—came again, and Soren stopped, every nerve in his body on fire, every hair on his arms standing on end. *It's not coming from anywhere ahead of me. Not behind me, either. It's…*

He raised his eyes to where the creature clung to the foam tiles lining the ceiling. Its jaws opened into a vicious smile, exposing rows of sharp teeth. Then it let go, dropping toward Soren.

GROWTH

A TAPPING SOUND STARTLED MARY. SHE DROPPED HER EMBROI-dery and crossed to the window, where Emma's wide smile was distorted by the glass.

Her friend beckoned, clearly wanting to speak.

Mary shook her head as she pointed back at the house. "I can't," she mouthed. "Mama will be home soon."

Emma wasn't deterred. She beckoned even more eagerly and pointed toward the lane bordering the property.

Mary huffed a sigh. "Very well, don't work yourself into such a frenzy." She snatched her bonnet off the side table and slipped through the house. The maids were all busy preparing for lunch. If she were lucky, her mother would stay late at Mrs. Crenshaw's, and Mary's absence wouldn't even be noticed.

"Lord, I thought you'd never come," Emma hissed as Mary joined her in the garden. "I've found something. Come on, come on."

Emma took Mary's hand, and she had to pick up her skirts to keep up with Emma's pace. "I can't be out long. Where is it?"

"In the forest. Don't worry. It's not far."

Mary tried to pull her hand back. When she spoke, her voice was a little harsher than she'd intended. "The forest? Are you mad? You know we're not supposed to—"

"It's only a little way in." Emma refused to lessen her grip. "You'll love it, I swear."

With one final glance back at her home, Mary huffed and allowed herself to be dragged toward the tangle of dark time-worn trees near the town's edge.

When they were children, she and Emma had played in the woods constantly. It was a wild land of hidden glens, streams, and seemingly magical clearings. But, eventually, both Emma's and Mary's parents had insisted they keep to the roads. "It's time to grow up," they'd said. "It's time to focus on worthwhile tasks, to better yourselves as young women, to give up the foolishness of childhood."

But it would be a lie for Mary to say she didn't sometimes daydream of the woods. Her protests to Emma were for show and to assuage her conscience, nothing more.

By the time they reached the wood's edge, they were both running, their cheeks flushed and their breathing ragged. Emma's eyes seemed unusually glossy. "Come on," she cried, leading the way between the thick black trunks. "It's only a little further."

"What are you showing me?" Mary's dress snagged on a

branch, and she gave a little cry as it tore. "Ah, Mama will be furious—"

"Never mind about that. Come on!"

This time, Mary flushed with anger. "What do you mean 'never mind'? I'll be in so much troub—"

"It's through here. Come and see!"

Mary pouted but obediently climbed the bank of rotting wood to see what Emma was so eager to show her.

Her friend knelt in a little hollow. Ahead of her was a cluster of strange fungi. Long and tapered like a lady's fingers, their bases were a green-gray and their tips yellowed. They were strange, Mary thought, but not so noteworthy as to justify a torn dress.

"Smell them." Emma bent close to the plants, her eyes glassy and her cheeks pink. "I've never smelled anything so delicious."

Reluctantly, Mary eased herself into the hollow. As she neared them, the fungi's aroma surrounded her. Emma was right; they smelled like honey, like freshly baked cakes, like lavender and cinnamon and apples and spring rain…

She was kneeling behind her friend and marveling at the plants. The dress no longer seemed so important. Being home in time for Mama no longer seemed important. She only wanted to sit and watch the fingerlike mushrooms for a little longer.

The sun was near setting when she shook herself out of her fugue. "We should go."

"Yes," Emma agreed. Her voice was slurred, and her eyelids half-closed. "In a minute."

"We can come back tomorrow," Mary promised. Only a vague

sense that she would regret staying much longer made her stand. "And the day after. But now, we need to go home."

Their walk back to the village was far more subdued than the dash away from it had been. They held hands but didn't speak, both lost in their thoughts and unwilling to break the trance.

As Mary had suspected, her mother scolded her both for leaving home and for tearing her dress. Her mother screamed at her, pointing to the grass stains on her knees and the leaves in her hair, but it didn't bother Mary. She only nodded when appropriate and apologized when her mother's silence suggested she was expected to. Her thoughts were still with the fungus.

She barely slept that night. She dearly wanted to go back to the plant, to see what it looked like at night, but she didn't think she could find the way in the dark. Besides, she didn't want to just see it herself. She wanted to show it to someone else. That was the purpose of pretty things, wasn't it? To share the joy with others?

Her mother had explicitly told her not to stir from her room the following day as punishment, but Mary only waited until she saw her mother's hat bob down the street below her window before dashing outside. She knew exactly whom she wanted to lead to the growth.

Her family, being one of the wealthier in the village, rarely spoke to the farming family near the woods, but they had a daughter around Mary's age. She found the girl tending to the chickens. It didn't take much to convince her to come to the forest.

"Where are we going?" the girl asked. Mary belatedly realized she couldn't remember the girl's name, but that no longer seemed important.

"You'll see," she replied, and laughed at how closely the conversation mimicked hers and Emma's from the day before.

The hollow already had a visitor. Emma was kneeling next to the fungi. Her hair was disheveled, and she still wore her night dress, but she didn't seem to care as she turned a dazed smile toward Mary. "Oh, you brought a friend."

Her fingers were sticky with a thick orange liquid. It looked like honey, but as Emma turned back to the growths, Mary realized it had come from the fungi. Emma had broken one in half and dipped her fingers inside. As she sucked on them, her eyes fluttered closed while she relished the taste.

Mary wanted to sample the plant, too, but some distant, subconscious caution held her back. *Don't eat anything that grows in the forest,* her mother had said countless times. *It could be poisonous.*

She closed her eyes and contented herself with the smell. The farmgirl had been mute, but very slowly settled beside her to be near the mushrooms. Her wide eyes were already developing a dull glaze.

Mary stayed as long as she dared, watching the little plants and listening to Emma lick her fingers. When she finally rose, the sun had fallen, but she felt neither hungry nor cold. Even keeping the same position all day had not made her sore. The farmgirl obediently stood with her as they turned back to town. Emma stayed.

Her time at home was a daze. Her mother screamed at her so violently that spittle flew from the woman's mouth. That didn't matter, though. The food passed through her bedroom door didn't matter, the hot bath didn't matter, and the starry night didn't matter.

Nothing mattered until Mary tried to open her door the following morning and found it locked. Then she screamed, shed hot tears, and beat her fists against the door. The doctor arrived. His diagnosis was hysteria to be treated with seclusion and a pungent herbal blend. Mary hated the medicine; it was so pungent, so bitter compared to her mushrooms. She swallowed it so that the doctor would leave her alone, then waited until her family went to bed before cracking open her window.

The cold outside air burned her throat as she ran toward the woods. She was barefoot, but the littered forest floor didn't hurt her. She wore only her nightdress, but the air didn't make her shiver. She followed the route to the fungi as surely as though the map had been branded into her mind. As she stepped into the clearing, she discovered the farmgirl had brought more friends. Five of them knelt in the hollow but didn't stir as Mary took her place among them.

Emma lay among the mushrooms. She looked so peaceful that she might have been dead, except for her infrequent, halting breaths.

The fungi had grown across her, sprouting from her skin in little pretty patches. Their gray-and-yellow stalks, so much like fingers, quivered every time Emma breathed. It was a sight that might have once filled Mary with revulsion but at that moment seemed natural and comforting. It was a good thing to have happened; Emma might die, but the fungi would live, growing from her collapsing body and spreading their sweet scent through the forest.

Mary no longer felt any of the niggling reluctance that had plagued her over the previous days. Her mind was pleasantly empty as she bent forward, snapped one of the growths off Emma's cheek, and lapped at the honey-like syrup that dribbled from its stalk.

QUARANTINE

THE SHUTTLE DOOR OPENED WITH A QUIET HISS. AVA PUSHED inside and floated in the zero gravity while she waited for Takil to follow her. He'd been unusually slow that afternoon, and she found herself crossing her arms as her partner drifted through the hatch.

"Anytime this century," she said, as he pressed the button to close the door.

She couldn't see his face under the helmet, but she could imagine the scowl he shot her. "Hey, shut up. It's not like we're on a deadline or anything."

Ava sighed and began typing commands into the control panel. "Yeah, sorry. You've just been... I dunno, like you've run out of juice. We've been working together for—what? Four years? And I can't ever remember having *you* follow *me* before."

The gravity normalized as the centrifuge kicked in, and Ava

let her boots drift to the floor. She pressed a second button to check the air levels were safe, then she unlocked her helmet. As she unzipped from her suit, she glanced back at Takil and felt a stab of shock. Her partner was pale and sweaty. He'd looked fine when they'd suited up, but something had obviously affected him during the four-hour flight. "Hey, is something wrong? You're not looking so hot."

Takil shot her a tight smile. "I don't feel great, to be honest. My wife was coming down with something this morning. I might have caught it off her. Don't worry about me, though. We'll be back to base in a couple hours, and I'll take the rest of the day off work if I'm not better by then."

"You sure? I can finish up here while you wait in the ship."

Takil punched her arm as he passed her, and opened the door to the small biotech room that held the life-support systems. "What did I say? I'm fine. We'll get through this faster if we both do it, anyway."

Ava sighed and hung her suit beside Takil's before moving to the shuttle's main control board to check for irregularities. It was a routine maintenance trip to an infrequently used midpoint shuttle, and if they were lucky, they could solve any issues within an hour and be back to their host planet early in the afternoon.

Her communication pad buzzed, and Ava unhooked it from her belt. Central's logo flashed on the screen, with her commander's insignia below it. She pressed the button to answer. "What's up, boss?"

Mal, her dark-gray hair slicked back above her deep eyes,

appeared on the screen. Ava wasn't sure if it was her imagination or not, but her boss seemed a little more frazzled than normal.

"Oh, good, you're there already. Everything going according to plan?"

Ava glanced behind herself, where the room was quiet and still. "Yeah, no problems so far. The system says there are only three noncritical bugs this time. Should be an easy job."

"Good, good." Mal glanced to the side, as though she were listening to someone beyond the screen's view. Ava tried to be patient. A call from her superior during a routine job was unusual, unless there was an emergency.

"Uh…" Mal glanced back at Ava and pushed a determined smile onto her face. "Just wanted to check that you and Takil are doing okay."

Isn't that what she just asked? "Yeah, things are fine. Should be out of here soon."

"Good, good, and neither of you have any sort of… symptoms?"

Ava hesitated and glanced at the biotech room, where she could see the bases of Takil's boots as he worked on the cabling under the water reclaimer. "Well, actually, Takil's come down with something. He said he'd probably caught it from his wife before he left."

"Ah." Mal turned to the side and spoke to the person Ava couldn't see. Her voice was too quiet for Ava to hear most of what she said, but Ava managed to catch, "Was she one of them?"

Mal's face darkened. She turned back to Ava, her smile

evaporated, and took a deep breath before speaking. "Captain Janes, there's a potentially dangerous disease passing through the stations. We have the situation under control at our base, but I suspect Captain Shamel may have contracted it before his deployment this morning."

Ava frowned at her boss, confused by the suddenly formal dialogue. She'd always gotten on well with Mal, to the point of being on a first-name basis and joining her for drinks on evenings when they had to work late. She wasn't sure what to make of the suddenly official tone. "So…should we come back straightaway?"

Mal paused for a moment before answering, and Ava hated seeing the creases building around her mouth. "No. Your orders are to remain where you are. Move Captain Shamel into quarantine immediately and avoid any contact with him. I'll send a medic crew to retrieve you as soon as possible."

"As soon as possible…" Ava glanced at Takil's boots, barely visible through the doorway. "How soon's that going to be? Within the next hour?"

"As soon as possible," Mal repeated then glanced aside. This time her companion's voice was loud enough for Ava to hear the urgent tones, but not the words. "Ava, I have to go now. Get Takil into quarantine, and stay safe."

"Stay safe?" Ava echoed, but Mal had already ended the communication. Frustrated, Ava clipped the box back onto her belt and scowled at the shuttle. "And where exactly am I supposed to quarantine someone on this heap of junk? Hey, Takil!"

Her companion didn't answer. Ava approached the biotech

room as anxiety began to flutter in her chest. Takil was kneeling on the ground, apparently lost in thought as he stared at the cables. Ava had to rap her knuckles on the door twice before he rocked back onto his heels and looked at her.

"Jeez," Ava said, lost for words.

Takil had looked bad before, but he'd degenerated to ghastly in the few short minutes they'd been separated. His hair was plastered to his face, which dripped sweat. His skin, normally a healthy bronze, had turned gray, and his lips were tinged blue. His unfocused eyes roved the room before settling on Ava.

"Huh?" he said, and a trickle of saliva ran from the corner of his mouth to mix with his sweat.

Ava swore and covered her mouth and nose with her sleeve so she wouldn't inhale any pathogens. *Is it a virus, though? I've never seen any sort of disease move this quickly.*

Takil keeled forward, and his hands flopped against his stomach as though to knock away an unpleasant sensation. Ava stared, transfixed, as her partner lurched back and his stomach swelled under his uniform. Fear fought through the confusion, and Ava remembered that she was supposed to quarantine her partner. She reached for the door to wrench it closed, but a second before she could, Takil's suit and stomach split open, spilling a series of long gray wormlike creatures onto the floor.

A scream rose in Ava's throat, but she choked it off before it could leave her mouth. Her partner rocked backward, his body collapsing against the network of cables, as the parasites that had grown inside him pooled forward, stretching toward Ava.

She slammed the door against them and stumbled backward, shock turning her limbs to putty. The parasites made wet, sticking noises as they pressed against the door. Ava skittered backward as far as the cramped room would allow her then dropped to the ground and pulled her knees up under her chin. She fumbled the communication unit off her belt and pressed the emergency button, then she stared at the screen as the little connection circle cycled around and around. *Their phones can't be that busy, surely? Unless this thing is spreading…*

She could hear the creatures moving. Their slimy gray bodies slid across the floor and walls as they searched for a gap to escape through. She didn't want to think about what would happen if—rather, *when*—they found a way out.

Please, Mal, send the rescue team quickly.

THE CLEANERS

"JEEZ, WOW." JERRY OPENED THE CAR DOOR TO GET A BETTER look at the three-story mansion towering above him. The day had been hot and sunny when they'd left the town forty minutes before, but thick clouds had blotted out most of the natural light and left him feeling chilled. "You've been coming here every day for the last week?" he asked, incredulous, as his cousin killed the car's ignition and undid his seat belt.

Ash gave him a toothy smile. "And been paid three times what I was making at my old job."

"How exactly did you get this gig again?"

Ash slid out of his seat and rounded the car to retrieve his supplies. "Craigslist. Put myself up as a professional cleaning company. No one checks your references, and it's simple enough to fake certificates and letters of recommendation. It's an easy job, anyway."

"Easy," Jerry repeated, staring at the building. "I'd call this the *opposite* of easy."

Ash, holding a mop and bucket in one hand and with spare cloths slung over his shoulder, gave Jerry's back a slap as he passed him. "It's not that bad on the inside. Just help me out for a day or two until I'm back on schedule, 'kay? Grab the spare boxes so we can haul some of the junk out."

Jerry rubbed at the back of his neck then sighed and retrieved the empty boxes before following his cousin up the weed-choked gravel driveway. It had sounded like an easy job when Ash had called him the night before. *I'm cleaning a friend's home, but I'm a bit behind schedule. Wanna help out for the day? I'll pay you fifty bucks.*

Of course, he hadn't learned until that morning that it was actually a paid job. And it wasn't a simple declutter-and-dust task, either. The elderly woman who had lived in the house had passed away a fortnight before, and her family wanted the building thoroughly cleaned before they put it up for sale.

Jerry swore under his breath and ran up the porch steps to where Ash had propped the door open with a rock. The foyer looked reasonably clean; furniture had been shoved into a corner, waiting either to be sold or carted away in a dump truck. An archway to the right led into an old-fashioned sitting room. Jerry's mouth dropped open as he turned in a slow circle, amazed by the opulence surrounding him. The gold-leafed sconces lining the walls matched the chandelier hanging high above his head, and the chandelier, in turn, matched the grungy marble tiles below his feet.

"This is incredible."

"It's sure something, huh? The guy who hired me said it was built in the eighteen hundreds, when the woman who lived here was a young child."

"What? Seriously? But wouldn't that make her, like, over a hundred?"

"That's what he said. I've got to finish in the kitchen—I didn't get through it last night—but it's a bit small for two of us. Why don't you head upstairs and pick a room? Just clear out any drawers, carry as much of the furniture downstairs as you can, and vacuum the floors."

"Clear out... What do I do with it?"

Ash shrugged as he backed toward the sitting room, dragging the mop in his wake. "If it looks super, super important, put it to one side. Otherwise, toss it all in the box to throw out. I already asked the owner, and he doesn't want any memorabilia kept."

"Right."

Ash disappeared from view, and Jerry was left facing the curved stairway leading to the second floor. He cleared his throat, picked up one of the empty boxes, and began climbing. The steps groaned under his weight, and Jerry couldn't help but wonder how long it had been since they'd been used regularly. *If the owner was over a hundred, she must have lived in the downstairs rooms, surely?*

The dark, musty hallway stretched ahead of him, coated in red wallpaper that had faded with age. Jerry tried the first door, but Ash had already cleared the room behind it. The second opened into a bathroom, which he skipped, but the third brought him to a cluttered bedroom.

"'Kay, you got this," Jerry said, clutching the box tightly. The room looked long disused. A huge wardrobe sat recessed into one wall, opposite a bureau, a small desk, and an empty shelf. Though the room had clearly been meant as a bedroom, it had no bed.

Jerry dropped his box beside the bureau and pulled open the first drawer, expecting linen. To his surprise, it was filled with piles of handwritten notes on aging yellowed paper. He leafed through a few pages, but the old-fashioned scrawl was indecipherable, so he dropped the papers into his box and went back for another handful.

A picture slipped out and fluttered to the floor, and Jerry bent to pick it up. It showed four women, all dressed in heavy Victorian garb and with their hair pulled back into tight buns, sitting in a semicircle. The picture was small and grainy, but the women all seemed to wear an identical inscrutable expression as they gazed at the camera.

He squinted at a shape in the background then lowered the picture to look at the wardrobe set into the back of the room. They were one and the same. The way the women were arranged around the wardrobe seemed to suggest it had some sort of significance. "Weird," Jerry muttered. He dropped the image into the box, where it landed on an ink-stained butcher's receipt.

Jerry moved quickly through the first drawer, dumping its contents into the box after a quick scan for obviously valuable paperwork. Halfway down, he came across a gold-embossed certificate. *Awarded to Miss Myrtle Vouchalis for exceptional contributions to the field of cryptozoology.*

Cryptozoology?

Jerry had heard the word before, though he couldn't remember what it meant. The certificate looked expensive and important, but if it had been left forgotten in a room that was never used, he couldn't imagine anyone still living wanted it.

Into the box you go.

With the top drawer emptied, he bent his head to check that he hadn't missed anything. Snagged between the base and the back of the drawer was a second photograph. Jerry reached into the bureau and plucked it out. What he saw set his heart thundering and sweat developing across his back.

The four women still sat posed around the wardrobe. This time, however, its doors were open. And inside was something Jerry couldn't even begin to explain. It was huge—taller than a human—and had multiple limbs extending from its elongated torso. Its head reminded him of an ibis's, except it seemed more like a skull than living tissue. Hollows filled the space where the eyes should have been, and the long thin beak stretched down in front of its body. The limbs were all scrawny and multijointed, like a spider's, and though it was hard to discern in the picture, the skin seemed leathery. Its arms had been spread out and fixed to the back of the wardrobe as though the furniture were an impromptu display case.

Jerry turned slowly to look at the dark doors set into the wall.

He dropped the photograph and took two steps toward the stained wood. "Ash?" he called, hoping his voice would carry through the old house.

"Yeah?" his cousin bellowed from the kitchen below.

Jerry fastened his sweating palms on the door's handles. "What's cryptozoology?"

"I know that… Isn't it, like, uh…"

Jerry pulled on the handles and tugged the doors wide open.

"It's the study of mythical animals, isn't it?"

Jerry didn't reply. He was captivated—and shocked—and amazed—and appalled—by the sight in front of him. The creature, standing nearly a foot taller than he did, remained in the wardrobe, its limbs still nailed to the wooden sides. Its empty eye sockets stared out of the birdlike head, and its leathery skin sagged about its ancient frame.

Jerry met the skull's empty gaze, and he could have sworn he heard a quiet rattle as the beast exhaled.

EXPERIMENTAL

ARLO STRETCHED THEN LOUNGED BACK IN HIS CHAIR. HE HAD his phone propped up against the back of the desk, playing that night's football game, and his ice pack had done a decent job of keeping the beer cold.

His shift at the Argent Research and Development Labs wouldn't finish for another hour, but it was the quietest part of his day; most of the labs had already been vacated, leaving just the deadline chasers and obsessives to burn the midnight oil.

Arlo's desk phone rang, jolting him out of his daze. He grabbed the receiver and tried to sound more alert than he was. "Arlo here."

"Hey," the voice said. "Everything okay down there?"

Arlo recognized the voice as belonging to the property owner, Mr. Chase. He carefully nudged the beer farther out of sight under the desk, despite knowing his boss couldn't see it. "Yeah, all good here."

"I'm going to need you to check on Dr. Beaufort on level four, west wing. I've had a couple of noise complaints. Tell him to keep the volume down, okay?"

"Sure thing." Arlo waited to hear the click as Mr. Chase hung up, then took his tools—a flashlight and a notebook—out of the drawer and tucked them into his pocket. Then he marched down the empty tile hallway to the elevators at the opposite end of the room.

As he waited for the doors to open, he tried to remind himself of who Dr. Beaufort was. He would have seen him every morning as the building's occupants filed in, and again every night as they filtered out. He ran through the faces he could remember, trying unsuccessfully to match names to them.

The elevator doors opened. Arlo stepped inside, pressed the button for level four, and waited for the elevator to take action.

The Argent labs were leased to a wide variety of industry professionals. Because of the location in the heart of the city, rent was expensive, and the labs had a reputation for housing some of the greatest minds of their generation. At least that was what Arlo had been told. All he saw was a lot of bickering and occasionally smashed equipment when an experiment failed.

As the elevator doors opened, Arlo snapped his fingers. He'd remembered Dr. Beaufort: the shortish man with a ruffle of graying-brown hair and a permanent frown. While most of the tower's occupants said good morning as they passed the guard station, Arlo didn't think he'd ever spoken to the scientist.

Arlo turned right, toward the west wing, and followed the

hall until he found Dr. Beaufort's door. To his surprise, the lab's lights were off. *Maybe he took a different elevator down while I was coming up?*

He didn't expect it to work, so Arlo felt a small shiver of surprise when the door opened with a nudge. As he stepped into the lab, he felt on the wall beside the door for the light switch and pressed it. The room stayed dark. *Maybe he overloaded the generator? It wouldn't be the first time it's happened.*

Arlo pulled out his flashlight and switched it on. As the narrow beam of light skimmed over the shadowed shapes cluttering the space, unease grew across Arlo's skin. It wasn't the standard mess. The lab was destroyed. Chairs had been overturned, expensive-looking equipment lay shattered on the ground, and the largest table had been crushed. Stains coated the wall closest to him. Computers had been torn apart. Arlo licked his dry lips and stepped into the room. Glass crunched under his shoes; he stepped back, then looked toward the ceiling. It wasn't a power outage, after all—the bulbs had been broken.

"Dr. Beaufort?" Arlo kept his voice low for reasons he couldn't fathom. "Hello?"

No voice answered, but as he held his breath, Arlo was sure he heard something stir deeper in the room. He moved forward cautiously, sweeping his flashlight over the debris and being careful to step around the broken glass and torn book pages.

He passed the largest desk and saw something under the smaller counter. It looked almost like feet. Arlo crouched so that his flashlight could illuminate the rest of the figure, and his breath seized in his throat. The familiar scowling face stared back, its eyes wide and wild, its skin horrifically pale. Rivers of blood dripped from where the back of the head had been torn away.

Arlo gagged and lurched backward. He bumped into something solid and turned to see one of the large reinforced crates he'd often seen the scientists shipping their live experiments in. The metal reinforcements had been bent, and a human-size hole had been punctured in the side.

"Oh…" Arlo turned toward the door just as something nudged it closed.

IN THE SPACE ABOVE THE WARDROBE

THE RAIN DRUMMING AT LAURA'S WINDOW NEARLY DROWNED OUT her cat's wheezing. Octavius, the ancient tabby, lay curled beside her pillow. Later in the night, as the temperature dropped, he was likely to burrow under her blankets to leech off her body heat.

"You doing okay, champ?" Laura asked as Octavius gave an extra-gurgly exhale.

He blinked slowly in response. The vet had said he was doing remarkably well for his age, and Laura had interpreted that as a gentle warning that she might not have her childhood pet with her for much longer.

She turned back to her phone and continued scrolling as she filtered through her Facebook feed in case anything new had cropped up. It was well past her usual bedtime, and she was procrastinating in the vain hope that the rain might stop so she could have an undisturbed sleep. When it rained at night, her dreams were always erratic and disturbing, and they often devolved into nightmares before morning arrived.

Octavius gave an extra-deep wheeze, and Laura looked at him. His eyes, fixed on something above her head, had widened into the perfect circles he usually reserved for when he begged for food or saw another cat on the backyard fence. Laura followed his gaze toward the dark patch above her wardrobe in the corner of her room.

There was only a foot of space between the wardrobe and the ceiling, which meant neither the room's light nor Laura's lamp were able to completely scatter the shadows there. Laura squinted into the darkness, but as far as she could tell, it was empty.

"What's-a matter? Seen a moth?" She gave Octavius's head a brief scratch.

The cat showed his front fangs, and a low rumble echoed from his throat.

Laura turned back to the corner, suddenly uncertain. Octavius really seemed to think something was there. Even though she couldn't see anything, Laura found herself focused on the area, matching her cat's gaze, as though a shape could appear in the thin block of shadows at any moment.

"Enough," Laura said, shaking herself out of the stupor and putting her phone back on the bedside table.

Octavius maintained his stare, and although she thought his tail might be a little puffed, he was no longer growling. "I don't know what's up with you tonight, Oct, but you'd better get over it. Good night."

She gave her cat's head a final scratch—not that he responded—
then turned off her bedside lamp and wiggled under her covers.
The rain continued to beat at the window, creating a strange
symphony with Octavius's thick breathing and the ticking clock.
Laura closed her eyes and tried to sink into sleep, but she was
excruciatingly aware that Octavious was still next to her and that
his wide eyes continued to focus on the shadowed corner.

Sometime during the next half hour, between the beating rain
and wheezing breaths, Laura fell into an unpleasant, disturbed
sleep. She dreamed she'd rolled over and opened her eyes to see
the creature crouched above her wardrobe.

It was entirely black, which allowed it to blend into the shadows
perfectly. Water dripped from its moist, leathery skin and ran
down the side of the bookcase to soak into the carpet. Its eyes were
the worst; they were large and round, with horizontal pupils, like
a cat's. They flicked from Octavius to Laura's sleeping form, back
and forth, back and forth, as hunger drew its lips apart to expose
the many rows of shiny white teeth packed inside its mouth.

Laura started awake with a gasp. It took her a moment to
remember where she was, then she scrambled to turn on her
bedside lamp and scanned the space above her wardrobe. *Empty.*
She sighed and rubbed her palms against her eyelids.

A low rumble from her side drew her attention to Octavius.
He was crouched in the space beside her pillow with his hackles
raised and his bushy tail curled around his body defensively. His
huge green eyes remained fixed on the corner of the room…the
space where she'd dreamed she'd seen the creature.

"There's nothing there," Laura said, more to reassure herself than to calm her cat. She looked back at the corner for the final time.

Something glistened on the side of her wardrobe. Water drops, catching her lamp's light, dribbling down the wood toward the carpet. Laura opened her mouth, but no noise escaped her.

Lightning flashed through Laura's window and dispersed the darkness in the corner of the room. The split second of sharp white light was just enough to illuminate the leathery flesh, the wide, hungry eyes, and the long shiny teeth hidden in the darkest corner of the space above the wardrobe.

ENJOY THIS SNEAK PEEK OF *FROM BELOW* BY DARCY COATES, COMING JUNE 2022.

No light. No air. No escape.

Hundreds of feet beneath the ocean's surface, a graveyard waits…

THE GULF OF BOTHNIA,
FORTY-ONE MILES OFF SWEDEN'S EAST COAST
THE MORNING OF THE FIRST DIVE

The camera's view blurred, then sharpened again to focus on a woman's profile. Cove Waimarie bent over a table, a wash of wavy black hair hanging like a curtain over one side of her face as she scratched in a notebook with a thick lead pencil. Behind her, the lounge's large plateglass windows filled the room with cool light. Foamy waves rose into view as the boat tilted.

"Hey there," Roy said from behind the camera. "Guess what? We're live."

She lifted her head, a mischievous smile forming as one eyebrow quirked. "Got it running, huh?"

"For the moment at least." He adjusted the camera, forcing the lens to refocus. Cove's form bled into the searing light behind her before shifting back to reality. "Did you want to do an intro, or—?"

"The day I say no to that is the day you need to put me out of my misery." Cove straightened and leaned one hip against the table, her feet crossing at the ankles. The ship rolled with every wave that passed underneath, but she showed no signs of losing her balance. Just like her outfit—white linen pants and a tan blouse that emphasized her warm complexion—the pose looked both comfortable and effortless.

"We're moored in the Gulf of Bothnia between Sweden and Finland, a day's travel from port. Somewhere in the water beneath us is a lost shipwreck that has both captivated and puzzled the world for decades. Why did it sail so far off course? What caused it to sink? Over the next few days, we intend to find our answers. How was that?"

The final question was directed at Roy, not the camera. He kept the bulky recorder propped on his shoulder but freed one hand to give her a thumbs-up. "Did you rehearse that, or does it just happen?"

"My father always told me to find a job that I love." Her smile widened, shining white against bronze skin, her green eyes filled with laughter. "And I love talking, so here I am."

"Well, there aren't many jobs that involve watching movies all day, but I got the next best thing." Roy flipped the camera and held it up to capture his face. The close quarters distorted his broad jaw and filled the lens with a view of thick, dark stubble. "*Making* movies."

A man's voice, dense with frustration, called from somewhere deeper in the lounge: "You're a camera technician, not a director."

"Ah, ah, ah." The camera rotated again, its view rocking wildly across the metal floor and cracked paint before fixing on one of the darker corners of the space. A man lounged in a roller chair, a circuit board held in one hand, screwdrivers and solders scattered on the table behind him. "That's our ROV wrangler. He was supposed to drop his little robots into the water and guide them down with a joystick. But just like with my film equipment, his robots went on the fritz sometime between leaving port and mooring. However, unlike my film equipment, he's been unable to bring them back online. Say hi to the camera, Sean."

Sean, with his buzzed hair and gaunt, heavily creased face, only glared at Roy.

"Some people would say it's a bad omen." The camera turned to catch another much younger man. He sat forward in his chair, legs flung out at uncoordinated angles, a mug clutched in thin hands. A batch of freckles—swelling thanks to the ocean's inescapable sun—covered his pale skin. He seemed faintly shocked that the camera was facing him, like a child caught trying to take a chocolate from a box meant for the adults.

"Say hi," Roy prompted.

"Hey." A cautious smile formed. Unlike Cove, he had

trouble making eye contact with the camera. "Um. I'm Aidan? I guess?"

"You guess?" Roy broke into heavy laughter. "If we're talking bad omens, I'd say forgetting your name is high up on the list."

"Sorry, I'm just saying." Aidan became aggressively preoccupied with his feet, tilting them in and then out again, his knuckles flushing white against the steaming mug. "It's kind of weird, right? The ROVs go out. The main camera and backup camera go out. Our navigation system glitched and sent us twenty miles off course…"

Cove crossed to Aidan's side and pressed one hand onto his shoulder, her other tucked into her back pocket. "You know, I like to think of it as excellent luck."

"Oh?" Roy lowered his stance to give the camera a better angle of Cove's smiling eyes.

"Yeah. Before, our plan was to send the remotely operated vehicles down for the majority of the exploration. Now? We get to do it. We're going to walk the *Arcadia*'s halls ourselves. That's pretty lucky in my books."

Aidan couldn't quite meet her gaze, but he couldn't hide a grin either. "Yeah, okay, that's pretty neat."

"As for the equipment malfunctions, Devereaux thinks we likely experienced a solar flare that damaged the more delicate equipment. The diving suit gear all seems to still be in good shape, and it sounds like Roy here saved at least one of the main cameras, so as far as I'm concerned, we're barely impacted."

Something clattered behind them. The camera turned just in time to catch a circuit coming to a halt on the desk where Sean had thrown it. The room was silent for a second, then Cove's voice returned, strong and encouraging. "Our dive isn't scheduled for another hour, and I've gone over the equipment so many times that my eyes have started to cross. Now might be a good time to introduce the team. What do you think?"

Roy adjusted the camera on his shoulder as he swiveled back to her. "Let's go for it. Speed run?"

"Speed run it is." Cove clapped both of Aidan's shoulders as she leaned close to him, tangling her hair into his. "You met Aidan. He's basically holding this whole show together."

His grin was growing more flustered. "I'm…I'm the uh…the assistant."

"He's modest." Cove shrugged. "He does everything from prepping food to assisting the rest of us with our work. *And* he's heading down to the ocean floor with us. Give him a few more years and he'll be managing his own chartered adventures. Now, we have Roy. Camera, audio, lights, all the important stuff."

Still behind the camera, Roy whooped.

"Hell yeah," Cove called back. "We have some really neat gadgets for this trip. Because of the depth, we'll have limited time inside the *Arcadia*, so we want to make the most of it. Roy's ensuring none of the cool stuff fails on us. Next up, Hestie, who is somehow able to read at a time like this."

The camera moved to catch the opposite side of the lounge where a thin, wiry woman sat with a paperback clasped in her lap. Her pale hair was aggressively, furiously curly, to the point where she used multiple scrunchies to keep it contained in a ponytail. Frizzy strands still spilled free, framing her face and pale blue eyes. She smiled at the camera, showing large buck teeth but, like Aidan, struggled to make eye contact with the lens. "I'm a bit queasy." Her voice was soft and Roy moved close to capture it better. "Just trying to keep my mind off it."

Cove made a sympathetic noise. "The first time my father took me onto a boat, I spent the whole time returning the seafood I'd eaten for lunch back into the ocean. Keep the ginger close and let me know if I can hold your hair back, okay?"

"Oh, I'm not... It's just nerves." Hestie cleared her throat, gaze flitting across the floor as she tried to find something to settle on. "Yeah. Thanks."

"Hestie's our marine biologist. She is *the* expert on the ocean in general and especially this region. We'll be going to her to identify every fish and sea sponge we spot."

The large teeth flashed back into view as she smiled, pleased. "Degree in biochemistry and microbiology, PhD in marine biology, postdoc in coral-plasticine interactions. Honestly, I'm just happy to be paid for something that relates to my career."

Aidan piped up. "I'm just glad to be paid period."

Both Cove and Roy laughed, Roy slapping the nearby wall for emphasis.

"All thanks goes to Vivitech Productions for that," Cove added. "Their sponsorship means the world. Not only do we get to explore this magnificent location but we get to share it with everyone else too, thanks to this documentary."

"Thank heaven we still have the cameras," Roy said.

"Speaking of technical equipment, we can't forget Sean—" Cove's voice cut off as the camera turned. Sean was out of his chair and shoving through the lounge's door to disappear into the hallways below. A woman, climbing the stairs to reach the lounge, pressed close to the wall to avoid being shoved.

Roy made a noise that was halfway between a scoff and a laugh. "He's just salty because he thought his ROVs would be the star of the show, and now they're bricked and he has nothing to do."

"He'll have plenty on his plate," Cove said, her voice still warm. "We all will. Our dive window is limited, so it's going to be a hectic few days. We haven't introduced Devereaux yet, but I think we'll save him for later and cut straight to Vanna, our diving specialist. How are we looking?"

Vanna, entering to take Sean's place, carried a dry suit draped over her forearm. Dark, heavy-lidded eyes scanned the occupants. She was a few years older than Cove, crease lines forming around her lips and between her eyebrows, and her short-cropped hair was swept back from large eyes and a broad jaw. She failed to return any of the smiles directed at her. "We should begin preparing."

"I love your timing. We were just about climbing the walls up here." Cove pushed away from the desk she'd been resting against. Hestie took a short, rasping breath as she put her book down and joined Aidan in trailing behind the camera as the crew followed Vanna into the deeper parts of the ship.

Outside, the ocean swelled, heavy with dark promises.

2.

Cove kept her feet light as she descended the narrow stairwell. The metal slat steps clattered under their shoes and the scratched, white-paint-covered walls seemed to squeeze inward, as though wanting to crush her.

She'd never gotten around to introducing herself to the camera, but that was fine; they'd need to record a separate segment later, maybe even back at the studio, that would serve as the film's introduction. Cove wasn't exactly a foreign face for documentary enthusiasts either, though she was still waiting on her chance to break into mainstream recognition and cement her place in the world as a conservationist and educator.

The company sponsoring them, Vivitech, had a reputation for short projects and cutthroat budgets, but they still had the capability to create an award-worthy documentary…as long as they were given the material to work with.

Who knew? Maybe this documentary would be the one. That all depended on what they found waiting for them on the gulf's floor. Something visually stunning, Cove hoped. Even better would be clues to what happened in the ship's final few days. Everyone, herself included, was desperately curious to know how an ocean liner could vanish so thoroughly on what was supposed to be a routine voyage. And Cove, more than the others, *needed* the expedition to be a success.

They turned a corner, passing the mess hall, and descended a second flight into the storage area where their dive suits were kept.

She'd spent much of her life diving, mostly at warm-water reefs, but this was her first venture into the deep ocean. She was qualified. Barely. Just like most of her team.

It was common practice in the genre of documentaries she hosted to overstate a situation's danger. *Pretty woman in peril* was a motif the studios liked, even when it was rarely true. Cove had stood within twenty feet of wild lions as she elaborated on the ferocious crushing power of their jaws—failing to mention that those lions were safari regulars that had grown up comfortable and lazy around humans. She'd hiked mountains in blizzards, speaking in a rushed whisper to her handheld camera about the early signs of hypothermia, even though a tour guide and her crew were off to one side and a helicopter was on standby to carry her back to her hotel for the night. She wasn't the only host to do it either. They were all competing to make their situations seem the most hazardous, the most adventurous, to remind those at home that there was still plenty of adrenaline to be found out in the wild, even though half the time "the wild" was twenty meters off a paved road.

Cove thought this might be the first time in her career that she wouldn't have to exaggerate the risk. Mountain climbing and wild animals and swamp waters were dangerous, yes, but deep-sea diving was an entirely different field. It wasn't even uncommon to hear of divers with a lifetime of experience perishing in familiar waters.

And she and her crew weren't just diving to the ocean floor. They were going inside a wreck. Cove knew what that meant, even if the bouncy lilt in her steps maintained that everything was fine. Going inside the wreck meant poor visibility. Narrow passageways. No one to help if they became trapped.

They had an experienced diving instructor—Vanna—but Cove still wasn't sure what to make of her. She usually found it easy to read other people and easy to make them like her. Vanna was a no-go on both. She'd barely said a word since they'd cast off from shore, and that was two days ago.

They reached the landing and Cove swung around to face Roy's camera. Eyes bright, smile warm, keeping her face at its best angle. "Through here's our storage room. We keep our diving equipment locked up tight when it's not in use. Check it out."

She stepped back so Roy could move the camera through the narrow metal door. Where they were, on the ship's lowest floor, was already technically underwater. The metal hull groaned as the vessel tilted. There was a strange, echoey hollowness to that level, and Cove couldn't help but feel that the ocean was already trying to suck them under.

"We have our food and fuel and spare bedding here too," she said, running her hands along the shelves as she approached the racks at the rear wall, "but we keep the good stuff over here."

The ship was technically larger than seven people needed, but the storage area still felt cramped and full of clutter. Roy, tall and broad-shouldered, was struggling to fit between the shelves without ruining the shot.

Vanna already waited by the diving suits. They had five in total. Two of their crew—Devereaux and Sean—didn't have deep-sea diving certification. Those courses, required for anyone who wanted to go below what was considered the safe limit for recreational diving, weren't common.

Cove loved the ocean, but a tight work schedule meant she could rarely make more than five or six dives a year. This would be her first unsupervised dive at those depths.

She was pretty sure she could say the same for Hestie Modise. The wild-haired marine biologist had spent substantial time in the ocean as part of her degree, but her dive log suggested she rarely dipped under the water when it wasn't professionally necessary. Cove supposed it was possible to love the ocean but not love being *in* the ocean.

Roy Murray picked up a range of work as a cameraman, and his experience around reef filming meant he spent plenty of time underwater, but generally only at shallow depths and in tropical regions. He'd rushed through his deep-sea certification to join the expedition, dragging Aidan along with him. Apparently they'd met during a vacation and become close. Cove had been seeking a cook-slash-assistant, and the timid, self-conscious boy tested well on camera, so she'd taken him. She was now starting to second-guess that decision.

If just one or two of them had been inexperienced, it wouldn't have been a problem. But collectively, they amounted to perhaps one and a half truly good divers. And most of that was down to Vanna.

"We're lucky to have Vanna Ford with us," Cove said, putting one arm around the older woman's shoulders. She felt Vanna tense and hoped it wouldn't show on camera. "She has over four thousand logged dives. A good part of that is open-water scuba, but her true passion is cave diving. Would you say that's right, Vanna?"

The woman's bony shoulders felt cold under Cove's arm. She let the silence hang for a painful second, then said, "Yes."

Okay. This part's going on the cutting room floor. Cove let go of her companion and leaned on the racks instead. "My crew's safety is always my top priority. What's waiting for us on the ocean floor is a veritable maze of tangled metal and tilting corridors. That's why we wanted Vanna: she's unparalleled in navigating tight spaces, having been recognized as one of the top cave divers in the southern hemisphere. Vanna, how do you think we're going to fare down there today?"

Vanna's heavy eyes narrowed a fraction, giving Cove the sense that it was a ridiculous question. She took a beat to respond. "Fine. If you follow my instructions."

"We intend to. Especially since we have these." Cove picked

up one of the helmets. "We're using full face masks. That means our breathing apparatus isn't connected to our mouths, leaving us free to talk through built-in radios. Not just that but these masks are fitted with some of the best underwater cameras. Two of them per person, in fact, with matching lights: a set facing forward and a set watching our backs. If a shark sneaks up on us, we'll catch it in wonderful HD."

"There won't be any sharks down there," Hestie piped up. She and Aidan had been so discreet that they'd blended into the background. Even Roy seemed to have forgotten they were at his back and had to do a strange hopping step to get them into frame.

Cove nodded encouragingly. Hestie darted her eyes to the camera and back, uncertain where to look, before clearing her throat. "Normally currents are constantly cycling the ocean's water, carrying in fresh oxygen and keeping everything, well, alive. But this is a bit of a dead spot. The Gulf of Bothnia has very slow water movement and therefore very little oxygen. There will probably be some old barnacles—we like to call them rustacles—but no coral and no fish."

"And no sharks," Cove confirmed. "I don't know whether to be relieved or disappointed."

"Suit up," Vanna interjected. "We're losing time and energy."

ABOUT THE AUTHOR

Darcy Coates is the *USA Today* bestselling author of *Hunted*, *The Haunting of Ashburn House*, *Craven Manor*, and more than a dozen other horror and suspense titles. She lives on the Central Coast of Australia with her family, cats, and a garden full of herbs and vegetables. Darcy loves forests, especially old-growth forests where the trees dwarf anyone who steps between them. Wherever she lives, she tries to have a mountain range close by.